A
Harlequin
Romance

OTHER

Harlequin Romances
by LILIAN PEAKE

Many of these titles are available at your local bookseller
or through the Harlequin Reader Service.

For a free catalogue listing all available Harlequin Romances,
send your name and address to:

HARLEQUIN READER SERVICE,
M.P.O. Box 707, Niagara Falls, N.Y. 14302
Canadian address: Stratford, Ontario, Canada.

or use order coupon at back of book.

MASTER
OF THE HOUSE

by

LILIAN PEAKE

HARLEQUIN BOOKS   TORONTO
WINNIPEG

Original hard cover edition published in 1974
by Mills & Boon Limited.

© Lilian Peake 1974

SBN 373-01831-2

Harlequin edition published November 1974

Printed in Canada

For my husband, who is!

CHAPTER ONE

'THE time has come,' said Jay, pushing away his empty cup and running his hands through his hair, 'for the two of us to face facts. We're not just "resting", we're unemployed. We've offered our services, our acting ability, our technical know-how, but no one wants to know. Together we've tramped round the agencies. In vain I've told them, when they've bothered to listen, that I'm not only an actor at heart, I'm an electrician, stage manager, make-up artist, floor sweeper even, if they liked. They're just not interested.'

Petra put her empty cup tidily in line with Jay's. There was, she thought idly, something comfortingly symbolic about their emptiness. Like their careers, they had at this point in time drained them dry, with no immediate possibility of their being refilled. She adjusted her hair-style, too, lifting it away from her cheeks so that it hung, corn-pale, just below her shoulders.

'At least you have a job connected with the theatre,' she said. 'At least you're working behind the scenes making sure all the lights go on and off at the proper time. You're not slaving away in an airless office — a different airless office every week — typing other people's letters.'

'Think yourself lucky,' countered Jay miserably, 'that you had the foresight to learn shorthand-typing before you surrendered to the acting bug. And think yourself lucky that when you go to the typing agency asking for temporary work, they welcome you with open arms. *They* don't turn you away with "Sorry, try again next week," like all the theatrical agencies we've been to.'

The café, untidy with its after-lunch clutter, quietened around them, as more people left, replete with food, than arrived hungry for a meal. Petra and Jay, facing each other, rested their elbows on the plastic-topped table and supported their chins on their hands. They gazed, not

7

into each other's eyes, but into the far distance, as far as the walls of the café allowed them to stare. They were attached to each other because of their shared disappointments; they were attracted to each other, too, but not deeply in love.

'When the show's over at the end of the week,' Jay mused, 'know what I'm going to do? I'm going home.'

In spite of herself, Petra's heart sank. She was fond of Jay, even if she didn't love him. If he had asked her to marry him, she would have considered it. Affection, she had heard, given time often grew into love. They had trained together as drama students, had been given small parts in the same plays, laughingly sharing their 'first time' experiences. They had tramped round the agencies hand in hand, seen the same heads shake, sometimes apologetically, sometimes aggressively, but always decisively, when they had asked the same question, 'Anything for us today?'

Jay was going home, and home to Jay meant something very different from home to Petra. She had only a vague idea of Jay's 'home'. It was large, he had told her, with a big, big garden, and cost a lot of money to maintain. She had often tried to encourage him to talk about it, but he would shrug off all her questions.

Petra's home was 'digs' wherever she happened to be working – in a theatre if she was lucky, in successive offices if she was not. Her parents lived in a modest cottage in the north of England, not far from Durham.

Jay's father, she had gathered, was a widower living abroad. Jay, who was Petra's age, twenty-three, had a twin sister of whom he seemed to be very fond, and an older brother, older by ten years. And that ten years more of living had, it seemed, given this brother the stature, in the eyes of his twin brother and sister, almost of a father figure. In the absence of their real father, he was the one they ran to for approval or refusal, for guidance and, most of all, for money.

And he was rich enough, apparently, to give them the money they asked for, provided he was convinced they needed – and not only wanted – it, and on one condition –

that they worked for it. What that 'work' was Jay had not specified.

Jay's brother's name was Alaric, Alaric Stoddart, and Jay's description of his autocracy, and his authority which no one dared to challenge, had not endeared the shadowy, distant figure to Petra. 'Thank goodness,' she thought, 'he's not *my* brother, and that I'll never meet him. I wouldn't lower myself to go running to a man like that for money!'

'What will you do,' Petra asked, 'when you get there?'

'Help in the house.'

'You surely don't mean – cleaning, dusting . . .?'

Jay laughed so loudly the other patrons turned and stared. 'It's clear,' said Jay, 'I'll have to teach you the facts of Stoddart life. So far I've kept it a dark, dark secret. I haven't wanted you – or anyone – to think me different. And in essence, I'm not. I'm just the same as any other struggling young actor. After all, I couldn't help the sort of background I was born into, could I?'

'I wish,' said Petra, 'I had time to hear your life story, but work – temporary though it may be – calls.' She found her handbag and Jay followed her to the street.

'Stay up late this evening, sweetie,' he said, kissing her cheek, 'and when the curtain comes down for the last time and I'm on my weary way to my flat, I'll call in and tell you a bedtime story. To a – comparatively – underprivileged little girl like you, it might even turn into a fairy story.'

'I can't wait,' said Petra, 'to see you wave your magic wand. Don't be too late, will you, or I'll be in bed.

Jay's eyes opened wide with masculine anticipation. 'I'll be late,' he said, and disappeared in the crowd.

Jay was late. Petra wandered about her living-room – she had rented it furnished with kitchen – disliking its drabness, turning her eyes from the threadbare chair coverings, the heavy grey curtains and the worn russet carpet. How much longer should she wait up? She pulled a book

9

on the art of acting out of her bookshelf and tried to concentrate on its technicalities and advice.

She waited until a quarter to midnight and got into her housecoat. She hoped Jay would not take it the wrong way. He surely knew her well enough by now to realize that she didn't act in private the way actresses were supposed by the press and public to act in private.

Jay was tired when he arrived, but infused nevertheless with an after-the-show elation. It was not necessary, he said, actually to face the audience to feel it. Even backstage you picked it up, like a radio receiver, the waves of excitement transmitted by the performers. Petra knew exactly what he meant. She had been behind the scenes so much herself lately — too much for her peace of mind and to the detriment of her acting technique.

She had admitted to herself long ago that she was not a very good actress. Leading parts never came her way. All the same, she had managed so far to make a reasonable living from the small parts she had been given by equally small repertory companies in the provinces. Only rarely did she win a part in a London production. It was, in fact, possible to count them on the fingers of one hand, with some fingers over.

Jay took the coffee she offered him, grumbling that 'it wasn't something stronger'. Petra told him it was 'strong' coffee and it would, she hoped, keep them both awake long enough for him to tell her his 'fairy story'.

'I'll begin,' said Jay, 'by showing you a picture.' He took it from his pocket and put it into her hands. 'My home.'

The photograph had been taken from the air and she looked down on a country mansion, vast, imposing, architecturally breathtaking, standing in a setting of woodland, shrubberies, meadows and lakes. It was, surely, a 'stately home' to beat all stately homes. It had turrets and domes, pillars and balustrades, ornamental figures perched on roofs, and columns supporting sculptured eagles, wings outspread. There were multiple windows, bays and quadrangles; gravel paths, fields with their cows and sheep, paddocks with their horses.

Petra looked at Jay and she could find nothing to say. 'Now,' he said, 'having deprived you of speech, I'll show you a brochure which will probably make you faint dead away. Then I'll have the pleasure of reviving you in the best theatrical manner.'

She flicked through the booklet. Galleries, lush with tapestries, corridors, ornate with statuettes, pottery and ornaments; state bedrooms, music rooms, dining-rooms and staircases peeled past her drunken eyes – drunk with the beauties which formed a rainbow of incomparable colours as they merged with the movement of the pages.

'Your home?' Deprived of breath, this was all she could manage.

Jay nodded. 'Together with my twin sister and my elder brother. And my father, whenever he condescends to show his face, which is very rarely. Brother Alaric's the heir to all those glories. For my part he's welcome. I'm a twentieth century man all through. I haven't got a feeling for history. My father's Sir Titus Stoddart, Baronet. That title will be Alaric's, too, one day. And man, he can keep it! I'd prefer to be plain "mister" any day.' He leaned forward. 'Notice the name of the house?'

Petra turned to the cover. 'Underlings.' She looked at Jay uncertainly. 'Isn't it – unusual?'

He laughed loudly. 'It's a joke. It was meant to be. A devilish old ancestor of mine called Sir Cecil Stoddart played it on his only son and heir nearly two centuries ago. The place was built – let me see, roughly late seventeenth century. It's been added to at various times, but it remains largely as it was originally built. It was called, simply, The Great House. It was a good description but lacked character. My old ancestor changed all that. Unknown to his son, he made a new will. The son's name was Alaric—'

'Which,' Petra broke in, 'your brother inherited?'

'He inherited more than the name. The first Alaric Stoddart was, according to legend, fond of the ladies. My beloved brother isn't exactly averse to them. His current girl-friend is out of this world. She's a model, but don't let that fool you. She's the daughter of an earl – her name's Yvette Duffey, Lady Yvette, please note. Jenny and I can't stand the sight of her.

'Alaric, my ancestor, went for actresses, one after the other. He never married them, but he did almost everything else. I'll spare your feelings and won't go into details. He was also a gambler and, as the history books say, a "wastrel". He loved good living, spent money with the enthusiasm with which he drank wine and to pay for his spending sprees, he "stole" valuable possessions from the house when his father was absent and sold them. I'm told he used to say, "One day it will all be mine, so I'm stealing from no one but myself." '

'But,' said Petra, 'he was wrong?'

'Quite wrong. His father, Sir Cecil, was so disgusted by his son's low moral standards, he banished him from the house. When the old man died, they found he had left his house to the servants, his "underlings" as he called them, the property and possessions to be shared among them! For a while, despite the son's efforts to win back ownership of the place, all went well. The "underlings" lived peaceably enough, dividing the place between themselves. But once the magic had worn off, the fight over the valuables began. There were so many evil doings – battles, trickery, murders and so on – the law stepped in and the reign of the "underlings" was ended. Those who were left were mostly women. Alaric saw his chance, ordered those women back to their kitchens and sculleries and he moved in, together with his latest mistress, whom he quickly married, and their four children. So the Stoddarts came back into their own again, although the name Underlings lives on. Its very name brings the crowds, and it's those crowds Jenny and I and a few others show round the house to earn our keep. It's almost Easter, which is when the season starts. Which is why I'm going home. To get myself a job, by the grace and favour of the present master of the house – my brother, Alaric the second.'

'And,' said Petra faintly, 'is your brother like his namesake?'

'My brother's a businessman to the core. He has a list of directorships as long as your arm, runs Underlings like a tycoon, rarely touches drink, but when he does, he can down it by the glass without a flicker. He gambles only on the Stock Exchange and then he usually wins, confines his "good living" to the necessities of life with a touch of luxury here and there—'

'Meaning women?'

Jay nodded, 'Women. He never goes on spending sprees, nor does he allow his twin brother and sister to do so. We have to earn our own living and only if we go to him on bended knee – not my line unless it's written into the script – does he put his hand into his well-lined pocket and produce a few coins. He lives up to his name. Alaric equals "all ruler", and rule he does with the so-called rod of iron.'

Petra took a deep breath. 'Does he like actresses like Alaric the first?'

'Actresses? You've only to mention the word and he rears up and paws the air.' He leaned back. 'No, definitely not actresses.'

'So he – wouldn't like me very much?'

Jay pushed his long brown hair from his forehead and studied her closely. 'If he could shut his eyes to your—' he moved his hands in the air, 'attractions; if he could look at your beautiful blue eyes without being moved by them, if he could look on your dauntingly high cheekbones and provocatively pointed chin and those luscious lips, without wanting to take you in his arms,' Jay laughed at her embarrassment, 'no, actress that you are, he wouldn't like you very much.'

Jay pulled her out of the chair and Petra tightened every muscle of her body. She knew what was coming. '*I* like you very much,' Jay whispered. 'You wouldn't—'

'No, Jay, I wouldn't,' she said, trying unsuccessfully to disentangle herself.

Jay sighed. 'If only I had the money, a steady nine-to-five job, a part in a play even, I could get really sweet on you. Enough to say, "Will you marry me?" ' He held her away. 'Would you, if I asked?'

She moved to a safe distance. Once, only an hour or so ago, in fact, she might have said, 'Perhaps.' But now she knew his background, his family history, his place in Society with a capital 'S', it was inconceivable that she could even think the word. Such a house, such traditions, such fabulous possessions that had been passed down through the ages – never, under any circumstances, even with a wedding ring on her finger and a marriage certificate in her hand, could she regard herself as one of the family.

'Sorry, Jay,' she said sadly, sad because she hated hurting his feelings, 'I could never rise to the part. Too demanding. I'm a bad actress, you know that. I'll never be the leading lady, either on the stage or in real life.' If, she thought, you could call his kind of background 'real life'.

He went to the door. 'Exit one spurned actor, looking suitably dejected. Underlings, here I come!' He kissed her lightly and went on to the landing. Petra closed the door and leant against it, then she felt it being pushed open behind her.

Jay stood there, eyes bright, smiling broadly. 'And you're coming with me.'

With a glass in her hand, Petra stood in the corner of a room. It was a large room in someone's house. It belonged to a member of the company whose play had just ended its run.

Jay had taken her to the party. As soon as it was over they were making for the Derbyshire hills – and Underlings. Petra's cases were packed and waiting in the boot of Jay's car. As she contemplated the half-inch of drink in her glass, she wondered at her impulsive agreement to Jay's suggestion that she should join him on his journey and at the end of it find herself a job, at his brother's expense, as one of the guides who took crowds of sightseers round the great house.

Jay had produced booklets, pamphlets, typewritten notes, all explaining in detail the history of the vast country mansion and its illustrious owners of past centuries. Petra had spent her evenings soaking up the information, speaking it aloud, rehearsing it as she would a part in a play. If she was going to work her passage, as apparently Jay and his sister were forced to do by the arrogant, autocratic master of the house and monster in disguise, then she was determined to train herself to such a pitch of accuracy he, her future employer, would not begrudge a penny of the money he would be paying her.

Now she watched Jay with some apprehension, as he swallowed one drink after another. She hoped that, like his brother, he could take it 'with barely a flicker'. He was socializing with something approaching desperation – he needed another job, a part in a play, an audition, anything to get him back on the boards as a wage-earning member of a company.

Sometimes this was, Petra knew, a better way of obtaining work than haunting the agencies. For herself, she had, for the moment, given up trying. There were ways, she knew, by which she could get herself a part, even – with the right man – a leading part, but those were precisely the ways which she had consistently refused to employ. If she could not succeed in the theatre on acting ability alone, then she would not succeed in the theatre. That, as far as she was concerned, was all there was to be said. Others had laughed at her for her high ideals, even Jay, but, she told herself, she was one who would not be party to the dwindling moral values of the times.

As she watched Jay he looked up, raised his glass, threw the remains of the liquid down his throat and put the glass down. He shook hands all round, any hand he could find, patted numerous shoulders, kissed every available feminine cheek and made his way towards the door. The winding path he was following was not due entirely to the human obstacles in his way. Petra could see that Jay, younger brother, could not take his drink as easily as Alaric the Ruler was alleged to do.

'Well,' said Jay, sighing himself into the driving seat beside Petra, 'I hope I've sown a few seeds. If just one takes root, there must surely be a part lined up for me before the sightseeing season's over.'

He reversed the car on to the main road, a dangerous procedure and usually frowned upon. There had fortunately been a short break in the continuous flow of traffic and they made their getaway with comparative ease and considerable speed, well over the limit set for the built-up area they were driving in. The drink Jay had imbibed had, without doubt, gone to his head and Petra began to dread the long journey through the night that stretched ahead of them.

Jay had claimed to prefer night driving. 'Less on the roads,' he had said when he suggested it. But Petra's watch told her that although it was after midnight traffic had not significantly lessened. It was not long before they left the town behind and were speeding on the open road. Each town they passed seemed a little quieter than the one before.

It was just after one o'clock that Petra noticed how slurred Jay's speech had become. He had not just mixed his drinks, he had mixed the drinks with fatigue and now it was telling on him, affecting his reactions and ability to go in a straight line. She was having no difficulty in staying awake. Fear saw to that, fear of the accident which seemed almost inevitable if Jay didn't pull himself together.

It happened as they were rounding a bend. Jay had slowed his speed, but not enough to stop the skid on the gravelly road. He lost control and the car slithered sideways. The tree came at them broadside on, hitting the left-hand rear passenger door until it caved in, smashing the glass and bringing the critically wounded vehicle to a standstill. On impact, the side of Petra's head had been rammed against the window – the safety belt had not held her tautly enough to avoid a sideways shift – and now she hung forward, stunned, limp and semi-conscious.

'My God, Petra,' said Jay, 'have I killed you?'

Slowly full consciousness returned and she found Jay's hand moving up and down the injured side of her head, like a horrified father trying to 'rub it better'. 'I knew,' she said thickly, 'I knew it would happen. I knew it, I knew . . .'

'Shush, sweetie.' He kissed her cheek. 'There's no skin broken, but you'll have a bump, a colossal bump.'

'The car?' she asked, her eyes closed, her head lolling forward.

'All right if I leave you a minute, sweet? I'll have a look outside.' In a few moments he was back. 'This, I'm afraid, is as far as we go tonight. The front's escaped, but the rear's in a mess, wheel buckled, door pushed in.'

'I must sleep,' she said, 'I *must* sleep . . .'

'I'll have to leave you, Petra. I'll get help, find the nearest phone box.' He reached into the back of the car, pulled a rug to the front, shook it outside to free it of broken glass and put it over Petra's legs. He removed his jacket, peeled off the pullover he was wearing, replaced his jacket and folded the woollen garment, making it into a pillow for Petra's head.

She was not even aware that he had gone. She had fallen into an uneasy doze. A long time later – centuries, it seemed – a voice said out of the mist, 'I've phoned Alaric. He's on his way. He's staying at his London suite.'

'Suite', Petra thought, 'not flat, not digs, not lodgings. But suite. Alaric the Second, Alaric the Great, yes, he *would* have a suite of rooms.'

'Where are we?' she slurred.

'About twenty miles from London. On the outskirts. Alaric said he'd phone the police for help when he's well on the way. Alaric said stay in the car until they come – that is, whoever gets here first. Alaric said he'd take you over, but I'd have to stay with the car till morning, and do the rest of the journey by train.'

'Alaric said . . . Alaric said . . .' What was this Alaric like, this man who ordered people's lives, who had under his control a positive goldmine in the shape of a great country house? Jay could say what he liked about his elder brother, but he could not hide the fact that he had a great respect for him, not to mention a great dependence on his judgment and advice. And his power.

Petra drifted off, as much to get away from the throbbing in her head as to sleep away her tiredness. Sleep left her abruptly, but she kept her eyes closed. There were two voices; one, placatory and apologetic, she recognized as Jay's. The other, terse, authoritative, clipped, she guessed belonged to no less a personage than Alaric Stoddart himself.

'What's the matter with the girl?' the unknown voice was asking. 'Knowing you and your female hangers-on, she's probably dead drunk. You do choose your women! I never did approve of your taste.'

'I can return the compliment,' was the brotherly answer. Then, 'Don't be a fool, Alaric, can't you see she's been hurt? Probably slightly concussed. When we crashed, her head hit the side. Knocked her out for a few minutes. I thought I'd killed her.'

The passenger door was jerked open – apparently the tree had bent it and it had jammed – a hand came out, fingers touched Petra's chin and turned her head sideways. Her eyes fluttered open and they stared into a shadowed face, only the lower half being visible in the light of the moon. She saw a long, straight nose, an unsmiling mouth with a sensually full lower lip, an uncompromising jaw leading to a firm, rounded chin. The eyes were partially hidden but appeared to be topped by thick, black eyebrows, a frown drawing them together until they almost met over the bridge of his nose. The rest of the man seemed tall, tough, broad-shouldered and intimidating, at that particular moment too intimidating for Petra, in her weakened state, to contemplate. She closed her eyes.

'Good God,' the words were whispered, after a long, dissecting silence, 'she looks like a ghost!'

Petra roused herself. She had to prove to this hulk of a man that she had substance. 'It's all right,' she muttered, sitting upright with difficulty, 'I'm not dead yet.' She jerked her chin from the pressure of the fingers and pushed the hair from her face with both hands.

The two men moved round the car to inspect the damage. The police arrived. Petra heard the words, 'breakdown', and 'tow it away', 'take your passengers'.

But the heir to the Stoddart fortune said, 'I'll take the girl in my car, thanks. I'm on my way to my home in Derbyshire. I understand she was going there with my brother.'

'Take the luggage, too,' said Jay. 'It's in the boot, which unfortunately seems to have stuck with the impact.'

'I'll take care of that, sir,' said one of the policemen, and take care of it he did, so well that a few minutes later the boot lid was levered open and five cases carried to Alaric Stoddart's large car, shining in the moonlight. The police car drove away.

Petra's door was opened again. 'Are you capable,' asked Jay's brother, 'of walking?'

Petra lowered her legs to the ground, lifting her chin and making full use of her dramatic training. She said with commendable hauteur, 'Of course I can walk. I'm not *dead drunk*. I was simply stunned by the crash.'

She stood, swayed and reached out for the nearest object, which proved to be the tree trunk of a body belonging to the master of Underlings. She was lifted without ceremony by the muscular branches of that tree trunk, and conveyed as if she were the sixth piece of luggage to the front seat of his car. Then, with the rug tucked round her by an anxious Jay, she was left alone.

While the two brothers talked, Petra had time to absorb, both visually and physically, the interior of the luxury car her future employer possessed. After the biting springs of Jay's front passenger seat it was heaven to melt into the yielding comfort of the cushioned softness beneath her.

She heard the muffled conversation through the open window. 'Money? Haven't you any of your own?'

'I'm broke, Alaric.'

'What, has she drained you dry? Haven't you learned to keep women in their place? You ought to know how to deal with them by now.'

'You can't bracket this girl with the rest. Financially,

she makes no demands. She knows I spend most of my time impoverished.'

'Don't give me that one. All women are the same. They're after two things and two things only – money and marriage, in that order.'

'This one's different.'

There followed a short, ironic laugh. 'No woman is "different". I'm too experienced in dealing with the female of the species to think otherwise. Does she know about your background?'

'Yes. I've told her everything.'

'*Everything*? Good God, man, you've had your chips. She'll cling until the wedding bells ring out.'

'Look, Alaric, I can't explain now. Circumstances all wrong, but I've got to have some ready cash for my fare and to get myself a meal. I'll pay you back, I promise. I'm coming home to work . . .'

Petra listened with tears in her eyes, tears of sympathy for Jay who was having to lower himself to beg from his wealthy brother, and tears of fury at that same wealthy brother's meanness and implied demand for his pound of flesh. 'Money and marriage', he had said, was what a woman wanted! With all her being she began to hate this man who was now, reluctantly, parting with some of the contents of his wallet to his pleading brother.

If she had the strength, if she didn't feel so dizzy as soon as her feet touched the ground, she would get out of the car and stay with Jay.

Jay, pocketing the money – there seemed to be a considerable amount – came across to the car and opened Petra's door. Alaric slid behind the steering wheel.

'Goodbye, sweet.' Jay took Petra's cheeks between his palms and kissed her lingeringly. 'Alaric will take care of you.'

Because his farewell seemed so final, because she was afraid of the long journey into the unknown she was about to take with this – this monstrous enigma of a man beside her, Petra clung to Jay and kissed him back.

'Don't be away too long,' she murmured, 'please hurry, Jay.'

Plainly moved by her unexpected outburst of affection, Jay said, 'We're not being parted for ever, pet.'

Still she clung – to the familiarity of him, compared with the stranger sitting stiffly beside her; to the kindliness of him, compared with the unsentimental harshness of his brother; to their shared experiences and struggles and the encouragement they had given each other when disappointment dogged them.

'You'd better uncouple the girl, Jay, otherwise you'll find her still hanging round your neck like Coleridge's albatross when the breakdown van arrives.'

Petra tore her arms away and jerked round to face the man who had mouthed the calculated insult. 'You—'

A hand was clamped over her mouth, Jay's hand, and it was Jay's voice urging restraint. But she shook herself free. Why shouldn't she speak to this man in his own terms? He was nothing to her. Master of his own house he might be, but he was not master of her! Then she remembered that, for the next few weeks at least, he was to be her employer, provide her with shelter, food and the other necessities of life.

She sank back into the breathing comfort of the upholstery and closed her eyes. Her head was throbbing and every movement jarred. This was a battle she would have to let him win.

'Thanks, Alaric,' said Jay, 'for your help and the loan. And for taking Petra over.' As though, she thought, I were a liability, a buck to be passed . . . The driver set the vehicle in motion, Jay with a wave merged into blackness and Petra cursed herself for ever having agreed to Jay's suggestion. She had wished herself on to a family which patently didn't want her. She had no place in it as either employee or friend.

They had been driving for many miles in the tautest silence Petra had known. It was well into the small hours and she longed for sleep, but kept it at bay without much difficulty. Not only was she determined not to reveal to this man that she possessed any form of human weakness, but the pain of the forming bruise at the side of her head was enough in itself to make the achievement of unconsciousness a virtual impossibility. She wondered if he intended driving through the night without a break. Was he so tough fatigue was an unknown sensation to him? Did he have such command over himself as well as others that he never lost control, no matter what the circumstances, never scaled the heights of ecstasy or floundered in wells of misery?

'How's your head?' The question was asked indifferently and without real interest.

'It hurts like hell!' The words burst from her, taking her by surprise, supplanting the platitudinous 'It's all right, thank you' that had involuntarily sprung into her mind.

He slowed down, saying coldly, 'In that case, we'd better do something about it, hadn't we?'

'No, thank you,' she replied with a coolness which equalled his.

His lifted a careless shoulder and speeded up again. 'What,' he asked after some time, 'and if it's not a rude question, do you do for a living?'

Again the innuendo, the malice which backed, like curtain lining, every comment he made relating to her. But this time she felt a spurt of pure delight, knowing how her answer was certain to arouse his anger.

'I'm an actress.' She flashed him a smile in the darkness, a smile of wicked pleasure.

But even his anger was muted. Instead of shouting, as she had hoped he would, he said between his teeth, 'An actress. Trust Jay to pick up one of those!'

She knew the expression had not been accidental, she knew it implied, in his 'shorthand' manner of speaking, that she and Jay were having a casual affair. The description of their relationship hurt. Her victory had been short-lived. She should have known better than to think she could win against this man.

Without warning he pulled into a lay-by. He slammed out of the car and opened the boot lid, returning with a picnic basket. 'Coffee,' he said, switching on the interior

22

light, 'weak, milky coffee so it won't stimulate.' He reached across her and felt in the glove compartment, bringing out a small bottle. He shook two tablets on to his palm. 'Take them with the coffee for your head.' Her instinct was to draw back, to refuse anything from him. He saw it and said, 'They're quite safe, simply an analgesic. They'll dull the pain.' She took them from his palm and examined them. 'I'm not aiming to dope you and abduct you. I'm no white slaver.'

She turned pale, reproachful, fatigue-wide eyes to his, but he merely smiled, knowing his shot had gone home. He unscrewed the lid of a flask and poured the milky liquid into a cup from the basket. For the first time she could see him clearly. He was dressed with surprising casualness, surprising for a man of his means and status, wearing a fawn cord velvet jacket with fashionable high-buttoning turnover collar, and tight-fitting cord trousers. His watch was different, too. It was large and plainly solid gold and was fastened to his wrist by a wide gold-band. Why should a rich man have less than the best?

On his right wrist was a silver identity bracelet, an effeminate affectation on many men, but on him it served to intensify his masculinity. His hair was jet black, with a deep natural wave which curved down over his forehead within an inch or two of his right eyebrow. He was holding out the cup and as she took it, their eyes met. His, she saw now, were grey, direct and keen, and as he lifted his cup in an ironic gesture, they were sardonic and mocking.

'Cheers, Miss – Miss—?' She supplied her surname. 'Miss Bain. Shall I give a toast? To the brevity of our acquaintance?'

'I echo that,' she replied fervently, 'the shorter the better.' Their cups touched and they drank, he with a faint smile, she with avidity to chase down the tablets.

'So,' he offered her a biscuit which she refused, 'you're an actress. Bain, Petra Bain. Can't say I've heard of you.' He glanced at her enquiringly. 'Perhaps you're – resting?'

'No. I'm out of work.'

He crunched a biscuit. 'Bluntness.' He said it as if he

were mentally listing her virtues and vices. 'Unusual in someone from the theatrical world. They're usually experts at evasion and prevarication.' He turned a sardonic look on her. 'Especially the women.'

She challenged, 'You don't like actresses?'

'I'll match your bluntness. No, I don't like actresses. And I refuse to bow to convention and say politely, "Present company excepted."'

'All right,' Petra said fiercely, banging her empty cup on the dashboard ledge, 'so you don't like me. I don't like you, either.' Then she put a hand to the bump which seemed to have swelled alarmingly. Anger was too strong an emotion for her injured head to stand. He watched her for a moment, then put away the flask and cups, and twisted round to place the picnic basket on the floor at the back.

'Anyway,' extreme fatigue overlaid with pain was making her sound childish, 'what's wrong with actresses? What harm have they ever done you?'

'None to me personally. To the Stoddart family,' he shrugged, 'possibly incalculable harm.'

'I know all about your namesake. Jay told me. But that was all a long time ago.'

'Agreed.' The car moved on to the road. 'But the odd weakness, if one can call it that, the strange partiality for such species lives on.'

'In Jay?'

'In Jay, but in my father, too.'

'Your father?'

'You know he lives in the south of France? That my mother died some years ago? He's filled her place many times over with actresses. He has a penchant for them. In the plural. Alaric, my namesake, was once the drain on the family resources. Now it's my father. The inherited tendency has skipped me – with one big jump – but seems to have settled squarely on Jay. Which is why I indulged his craving for the stage by letting him go to drama school. I hoped it would get the whole thing out of his system. It hasn't, of course. Yet.'

'Wasn't that rather a strange decision on your part? As

a drama student and now as a fully-fledged actor, he's been mixing freely with his opposite number – actresses.'

'I'm beginning to see that perhaps the entire venture was a miscalculation on my part. He is indeed "mixing freely with actresses".' He gave her a quick, unflattering look. 'Judging by his behaviour towards you, as I saw for myself earlier, a great deal too freely.' He paused, to negotiate a roundabout. 'No wonder he had to ask me for money.' He muttered, 'The rot has begun to set in already.'

'Yes,' said Petra furiously, 'vampire that I am, I'm drinking him dry of cash daily. It won't be long now, will it, before he starts "borrowing" the valuable paintings and priceless ornaments from his home and selling them to pay off his debts like his and your "wastrel" of an ancestor, Alaric the First.'

He laughed. 'And I'm Alaric the Second?'

'Yes,' she said, elaborating unguardedly, 'King Alaric, "Monarch of all you survey".'

He took her up, softly, 'Finish the quotation – "*My right there is none to dispute, From the centre all round to the sea, I am lord of the fowl and the brute.*"'

'Hadn't you better add,' she said sourly, ' "and women"? You see, Jay has told me about that, too.'

'Lord of women? Yes,' mockingly, 'the idea appeals. So I have a reputation for pursuing the opposite sex?'

'Yes,' she snapped, 'rumour has it that you have an unmistakable *penchant* for them. Except actresses.'

'You're so right,' he drawled. 'I cannot stand actresses.'

'At any price.'

'No, not even within touching distance.'

She drew away from him. She was sure he was smiling as he thrust the car into the wall of darkness which stretched ahead, always ahead of them.

'The compliment's returned. I can't stand lords of manors, especially those who keep their younger brothers in comparative poverty, only handing out insulting amounts of pocket money when begged to do so.'

'If you're talking about my brother,' came the quiet reply, 'with due respect, it's hardly your business. In any case, Jay is over age – five years over – and should by now be capable of standing on his own feet financially, without help from me. Especially as I poured so much money into his training at drama school.' He looked at her. 'He didn't tell you that, did he?'

'All the same,' she refused to acknowledge it was a considerable point in his favour that he had given Jay financial backing as a student, 'you don't know how hard it is to get an acting job nowadays, even if you're good.'

'Which you aren't?'

'No, I'm second-rate.'

'That wouldn't be false modesty on your part, of course?'

She resented the sarcasm. 'No, it's not! I'm a terrible actress.' She felt swamped by self-pity and fought a startling desire to cry. 'I can't get a job because there's always some girl who can do the part better. And I'm being perfectly honest. If you don't recognize sincerity when you see it, then for a businessman you're very undiscerning, with a warped, distrusting mind!'

She was by now hardly aware of what she was saying, although something inside her tried to warn that, in speaking to this man, she should speak with more respect. But her watch told her it was nearly four o'clock. Her body told her she should have been asleep hours ago. The pills she had taken had dulled the pain in her head, but the ache, although muted, persisted still.

'No one,' he said softly, into the silence, 'has ever spoken to me as you have done.'

If it was a warning, she ignored it. 'Then it's high time someone did. No human being can set himself above criticism. You might be master in your own house, but I'm not one of your lackeys.'

By his swift, hissing breath she guessed hazily that she might now have gone too far, but her mind was confused. Her two hands clamped to the sides of her head didn't stop the car revolving. 'I'm sorry,' she said weakly, 'but I

26

feel terrible.'

She heard him mutter something about delayed shock, but he said aloud, 'It's time we both relaxed, you most of all.' He drove on for a few minutes, then turned sharply left, Petra guessed on to the verge beside the road. Seconds later she was being lifted and carried, and set down with surprising gentleness in the back seat of the car. The rug, Jay's rug, was tucked round her and she opened her eyes to see Alaric remove his jacket, fold it and put it behind her head.

He closed the door, disappeared and reappeared the other side, getting into the back to share the seat with her. He folded his arms, increased the distance between them by shifting as far away from her as possible, rested his head against the padded side of the car and closed his eyes. He had no covering, no jacket even, and the night was far from warm. Momentarily she felt sorry for him, but she checked the emotion as soon as she became aware of it. She wouldn't allow herself to feel sorry for such an arrogant man. Let him experience a few of the discomforts of life, it would do him good.

She settled into her corner only to realize with some dismay as she nestled against his jacket that it was the injured, throbbing side of her head she was leaning against. She moved his jacket behind her and let her head flop backwards, but it was too uncomfortable to tolerate. He opened his eyes and watched as she moved his jacket yet again so that it pressed against the uninjured side. But she felt herself slipping slowly, inevitably towards him. Hopelessly she sat up and the folded, rather maligned jacket slipped down on to the seat between them. They stared at each other in the faintest hint of the approaching dawn.

'There's only one thing to do, isn't there?' He patted his shoulder. 'Rest your "pillow" against this, then we might both of us get some peace.' She drew away as if the thought itself was poison being offered to her to drink. 'For God's sake, girl,' he said, showing anger at last, 'you can surely overcome your dislike of me enough to use me as a support. Heaven knows, dozens of others do without a qualm, so I'm used to it.'

He refolded his jacket and put it against him. Delicately she rested her head on it. A sigh escaped her, of relief, of sudden, inexplicable peace. She slept.

CHAPTER TWO

CONSCIOUSNESS returned slowly a few hours later. With her eyes closed, Petra listened, wondered and – above all felt. She felt the warmth and steady breathing of a man beside her. 'Jay?' she whispered, and the question drifted through the partly open window to mingle with the joyous chorus of bird song.

At first there was no reply. Her head was resting against a hard chest, an arm was round her. The body against which she was snuggling, so confidently, so comfortably, stirred, then was still.

'No,' said a dry voice over her head, 'I'm not Jay, although I've no doubt it's he you're so accustomed to waking up and finding beside you every morning.'

She stiffened, but the arm which was round her stayed firmly where it was. She moved her head so that she could see him. He was wearing his jacket – somehow in the night he must have got himself into it without waking her – and he was staring out of the window. They seemed to be parked in the entrance to a farm gate. The rug was across them both. There was dark stubble on his chin, but otherwise he looked cool and collected. She said, urgently because of an odd need to convince him, 'You've got it all wrong.'

His head turned slowly and he looked down into her reproachful eyes. 'Have I?' His voice was dry and it was plain he didn't believe her.

Fighting the strong desire to remain where she was – she must still be tired, she decided – she lifted herself away from him and he removed his arm. Embarrassment brought a stumbling apology to her lips that she had forced herself on him. He said dryly, 'Not at all, I asked for it.'

That, she reflected, could be taken in two ways. First, that he had actually invited it; second, that he had brought it on himself unintentionally and against his will.

She had no difficulty in deciding which of the two he had meant.

Her hand went agitatedly to her hair. She hadn't looked in a mirror for hours. 'I must look a mess.'

'M'm.' He regarded her mockingly. 'You do have a touch of the debauched about you. You'll have to do something about that before we get back into polite company, otherwise I'll be blamed and be forced by the elevated social circles in which I sometimes move either to make an honest woman of you by marrying you forthwith or buy you off with a handsome sum to get rid of you. After all, we have – literally – slept together.' He cut off the gathering storm of her reply by asking, 'How is your head?' He touched it.

She moved out of reach. 'There's a large bump, but it could be worse.' She frowned and sought his eyes. 'Is it – would you mind telling me if it shows?'

Obediently he looked over the area of the bump. 'No, it doesn't spoil your looks.'

'I haven't any to spoil.'

He sighed. 'If you're fishing for compliments, I'm sorry, it's too early in the day to rise to the bait.' He felt his chin. 'I imagine I have "the morning after" look, too.' He got out. 'Do you want to join me in the front?'

'Yes, please.' She folded the rug and put it on the seat. He opened the door and motioned her towards the front of the car. 'I'm flattered. After spending the night with me, I'm surprised you still want my company.'

As her legs took her weight she swayed and his arm came out to steady her. He helped her into the front seat. He smiled. 'As a member of the acting profession, I would have thought you'd have learnt to take your drink better than that!' He settled himself in the driving seat. 'Incidentally, had you been drinking before I met you?'

She resented his question and showed it. 'Jay took me to a party. I had *two* drinks.'

'And Jay?' She was silent. 'It's all right, I know my brother. He was loaded with the stuff, which is why he had the accident. In the circumstances, it was lucky it was not a great deal worse.'

With the coming of the morning, Petra's spirits had risen. Daylight had brought sunlight which in turn brought optimism tagging along behind it. This man might be a monster, but he was a human monster. She could tolerate him as an employer for as long as it was necessary to carry out the job as guide to the inquisitive hundreds who would pass from Underlings' 'Entrance' to Underlings' 'Exit'. He would be the provider of her bread and butter and perhaps a bit more besides. It might be strenuous and even tiring, but she would, Jay had assured her, have a comfortable bed to sleep in – she should see the spare room, never used, in Underlings – and it was far better than typing all day, with a different employer every week.

He broke into her thoughts. 'What was Jay intending to do – drive through the night?'

She answered indignantly, detecting criticism, 'Well, you did, didn't you?'

'Yes, but I left home stone cold sober, and have remained so throughout the journey.'

'Jay couldn't help himself. You can't go to a theatrical party and shake your head every time someone offers you a drink.'

'If your story that you only had two is true, you must have done, many times.'

'*I* wasn't desperate for a part like Jay, so I stood in a corner and watched.'

'But why?' He seemed honestly surprised. 'You told me you're out of work.'

'I am, but I've given up trying for the present.' She gazed at the passing scene. 'I suppose in a way I've lost hope. I told you, I'm not "leading lady" material.'

'Is it polite to ask what you've been living on?'

She said fiercely, resenting his insinuation, 'Money that I've earned working as a shorthand-typist.'

'That must have grated.'

'It did. I hated it.'

'So you've given it all up and thrown in your lot with Jay?'

She was about to ask him what he meant when he signalled that he was turning left and pulled into the fore-court of a large, expensive-looking hotel. 'We'll breakfast here and wash, shave, change, whatever you wish. Have a bath, if you like.'

'But,' she was bewildered, 'have we much farther to go?'

'About seventy miles.'

'Then couldn't we wait until we got—' she checked herself.

'Home?' he mocked. 'You're not married to my brother yet.' With which curious statement he got himself out of the car and held her door open. She stood beside him, staring at the building he intended them to enter. 'What's the matter?' he asked. 'Isn't it good enough for you?'

'*Good* enough? It overwhelms me. My experience of hotels has been strictly limited to AA Approved, and then only on special occasions.'

'This,' he said casually, 'is four-star. Take heart, they know me here. I've been before, both with and without a woman companion.

She coloured deeply and turned back. If that was what they were going to think of her ... 'You go in,' she said, 'I'll wait in the car.'

He grasped her wrist. 'Don't be so stupid. If it's going to worry you that much, although with the experience of shared hotel bedrooms you as an actress must surely have, it beats me why, I'll introduce you as my future wife.' He examined her hands. 'Are you wearing a ring? Most women do. Yes,' before she could stop him he had pulled off the ring from her right hand. Without ceremony or gentleness he pushed it on to her engagement finger.

'The ring's worthless,' she objected. 'It was bought for next to nothing at a department store.'

'Worthless or not,' he said irritably, 'it makes you look the part.'

Still she objected, looking down at her creased, well-worn trousers and white, high-necked sweater. 'I can't go into a place like that looking like this.'

'Don't worry, hotels are used to all sorts,' he glanced at her critically, 'even women who look as if they had spent

32

the night with a man in the back of a car, which is precisely what you've done. Although,' he taunted, 'if you'd been with Jay, you would have made much better use of it than we did.' He grasped her wrist again and pulled her towards the entrance. She said plaintively that he was hurting her.

'If you promise to come quietly, I'll let you go. Good heavens, you were trained as an actress, which should surely help you to carry off most situations with reasonable poise, even if you're quaking inside. Isn't that what drama school's all about?'

The receptionist, a mature, well-built blonde, greeted Alaric with cheerful respect. That she knew him was evident; that she admired him was plainer still. Petra, watching as he spoke to the woman, could not deny the attraction of his good looks and his powerful physique, the charm he kept well hidden, but which was apparently devastating if he ever chose to use it. This he was doing now, to some purpose. The receptionist glowed under his winning smile.

'A room,' she said, 'for an hour or two for yourself and your fiancée? Double, with bath? Certainly, sir. Any cases required?'

He turned. 'Want a change of clothes, Petra?'

Her heart jolted as he called her by her name. But of course he couldn't say 'Miss Bain' to his 'fiancée'. All the same, she could not bring herself to call him Alaric, so she answered, 'Yes, please. My blue case.'

He handed the key to the porter, telling him the car's registration number. 'I'd like the red case, too. It's labelled with my name.'

As they waited, Petra wandered round the soft-carpeted, slipper-silent foyer. Everything was subdued, the décor, the lighting, the voices of the guests. Glass cases held tantalizing merchandise – wispy scarves, delicate perfumes from abroad, fabulous jewellery. Petra lingered, admired and longed.

Alaric came to her side. 'Does anything suit your taste?'

She sighed, her breath making a misty patch on the

protective glass. 'All of it.'

'And what are you going to buy?'

'Buy?' Her frown met his smile. 'I couldn't afford a single thing, you must know that.'

'Then why are you tantalizing yourself by looking?'

'Human nature, I suppose. One often looks with longing at things one knows will never be yours.' She smiled slightly. 'But you, of course, can't possibly know that. You're so rich, you've only got to produce your wallet and anything you want could be in your possession in a matter of moments.'

'Really?' His hand reached to his inside pocket and he held up his wallet. 'If I offered you the contents of this, would you become mine, "possessed" by me?'

Her own face frowned back at her from the reflecting glass of the case. 'No. I'm not for sale.'

The swing doors swished and the porter came in carrying the two cases. 'No?' Alaric whispered in her ear. 'Don't you believe it. Every woman has her price.'

'You,' she hissed, 'know all the wrong women. I'm different.'

'Which is what Jay called you. But I know I'm right and, given time, I'll prove it. As I said before, no woman is "different".'

'Your keys, sir.' The porter handed them back. 'Which room number, sir?'

Alaric told him and motioned Petra up the stairs in front of him. The bedroom was one of the most luxurious Petra had ever seen. The double bed was covered with a deeply quilted flame eiderdown. The carpet was soft-piled and off-white. There were two of everything – wardrobes, chests of drawers, dressing-tables, even writing desks and telephones. She wandered breathless into the bathroom. It was pale blue tiled, the blue bath was sunken, there was a shower; mirrors all round showed her herself from all angles and she closed her eyes in despair. Was that what she looked like? No wonder Alaric Stoddart had been making such caustic comments about her appearance!

She lifted her hair to inspect her bump. He came in at

that moment and examined the injury, too. Gently his fingers pressed and she winced. 'It still hurts?' he asked.

'Yes,' she answered briefly, and walked away. She could not stand having the man too near. In the centre of the palatial bedroom, she stood still. 'Isn't all this unnecessary expense? Couldn't we have patronized a petrol station and used the cloakrooms? I could have washed and changed when we arrived at your – your place.'

'My "place", as you put it, is a little more complicated than you seem to think. You've never seen Underlings, you know nothing about it.'

'You're wrong. I know pretty well everything there is to know – its dimensions, its traditions, its history, its past owners, the dates of their births and deaths.' What am I doing? she wondered. Talking myself into the job? Acting as my own agent, providing my own testimonial?

His eyes narrowed as she spoke. He did not seem as pleased as she thought he would. Had she sold herself short? Should she try again to convince him that she was quite equal to the position of guide, had learned her lines as if she were about to tackle the most important acting engagement of her life?

'One of the reasons for taking this room,' he said curtly, 'was to ask you a few questions. Your answer to those questions will be, to me, to put it mildly, illuminating.'

'But,' she wanted to say, 'it's only while the season lasts. By then I hope to have found myself another acting job.'

He said, 'However, first things first. I imagine you want to change?' He pointed. 'Your case. The bathroom, in which you will find towels. While you bath, I'll shave in here. When I've had a bath, we'll talk.'

So, Petra thought, the interview was yet to come. The job was not hers for the asking as Jay had implied. If his brother thought her unsuitable, what then? Her heart sank, but as she locked the bathroom door, undressed and stepped down into the soft, Mediterranean blue water, her heart rose again and floated, with her spirits, buoyantly on the perfumed air around her. She wallowed in the luxury, she couldn't help it. It would never come her way again. Who could blame her for taking it with open arms? If this was what affluence could buy, even for an hour or two, then who was she to spurn it?

The towel was soft, caressing and enormous. With the help of the talc that had been provided so thoughtfully by the management, she dried in record time. She slipped into the skirt and floral blouse she had taken from the case. The outfit was neat and simple, the skirt fitting well over her slim hips. Her feet would be cooler in the heelless sandals and her hair, which she fixed back with two pink slides, left her face uncluttered and revealed.

'I look what I am,' she thought disparagingly, 'an impecunious young actress, waiting expectantly on the sidelines for the leading part which refuses to come my way.' Never, however long she might live, would she be able to rise to Alaric Stoddart's standards of femininity. She hadn't the poise or the polish he would look for in a woman.

When she returned to the bedroom he was staring out of the window. She saw with an odd shock that he was stripped to the waist. A towel was flung carelessly over one shoulder and his hands were on his hips. He turned and she saw the mass of fine black hair on his chest and which covered his arms down to his wrists. She felt a frightening pull inside her as if his intense masculinity was reaching out, magnetwise, to trap her.

'I notice,' he said with a mocking smile, 'that you locked the bathroom door. Didn't you trust me?'

Trust him? Her impulse was to say 'No, being a woman I wouldn't trust you within a mile of me.' But, she thought, trust this man, with his tough exterior, his rough tongue, his hard, cynical manner? Wasn't there something more to him, a quality lurking beneath those sardonic eyes which could not be doubted, however hard one tried? Wasn't there an integrity, a reliability which, when appealed to, would never let one down?

She produced a nonchalant shrug from the mire of uncertainty which was sucking down her composure. 'Trust you? How can I tell? I'm not well enough acquainted with you to know.'

He said, looking into her face, 'We can soon alter that.' He took up a handful of clothes and went into the bathroom, but she did not hear him lock the door.

As she applied her make-up – doing it with the skill her present part in this odd play she was acting in required – she wondered what he meant. How, when he became her employer, did he intend to set about getting 'better acquainted' with her?

When he returned from the bathroom, he had abandoned his roll-collar shirt for a more conventional style, but it was unbuttoned to the waist. Reflected in the dressing-table mirror, Petra saw him watching her as she put the finishing touches to her make-up. Embarrassed, she picked up a comb and flicked it through her hair.

She turned questioningly, wondering why she was an object of such interest to him – he must surely have seen women, many women, applying cosmetics and making themselves look attractive, not, as in her case, to impress him with her potential as an employee, but to make themselves more desirable to him.

He looked her over and there was something in his expression which disturbed her. He was plainly not seeing her as she wanted him to see her, and as if to prove her point, he threw himself full length on the bed and put his hands behind his head. He did not close his eyes, instead he narrowed them and watched for her reaction. It was nil.

'Comfortable bed,' he murmured. He patted the empty space beside him. 'Try it.'

Was this what he had had in mind when he said they would soon become 'better acquainted'? She had become so stiff, her breathing so shallow, her lungs were fighting to function. His dark good looks, the incredible magnetism which he seemed to be able to use to trap women as undersea creatures use malevolently subtle lures to entice their prey began to close around her like a net. Was his dredging operation going to succeed? Had he entangled her enough to start pulling her in?

She saw the speculation in his eyes, the tentative assessment as to how much more inducement he might have to employ to persuade her to accept his invitation. She turned away sharply. 'No, thanks. I'll take your word for it.'

A question came softly, 'Do I repel you?'

A long pause, then, 'Not exactly.'

'Is it because I'm not Jay?'

What was the motive behind this subtle inquisition? After a long silence she replied, 'I know you won't believe me, but – I'm a naturally fastidious person.'

'You mean you're choosy about whom you allow to share your bed?'

'I meant nothing of the sort. I knew you wouldn't believe me.'

He leaned on his elbow and traced the intricate stitching on the eiderdown on which he was lying. 'I thought it was the habit of all actresses to seize any and every opportunity for getting a part, no matter how much it cost them in self-respect? And that therefore you must be no stranger to a situation such as this?'

'I told you, I'm an out-of-work actress. Doesn't that prove my point?'

But he would not be convinced. 'All the more reason, surely, for using the old accepted methods?' She pursed her lips and turned away.

Outside in the hotel gardens, guests were wandering about, some with cameras, others leading their dogs, couples holding hands. How straightforward life was for some people, she thought, looking out at them with powerful envy. She would give a great deal to be down there, wandering as they were doing, soaking up the spring sunshine, at liberty, free, free from the tentacles that were reaching out to her from that luxurious bed – and the man who, for the moment, had made it his own.

'Is it,' he repeated quietly, as if he was determined to have his answer, 'because I'm not Jay?'

'Jay,' Petra said, her fingers gripping the window-sill, 'is sweet, considerate and unselfish, and I'm very fond of him, but no, it's not because you're not Jay.'

The man on the bed swung his legs to the floor. He picked up the phone and dialled reception. 'Will you send up breakfast for two, please, to room twenty-one?'

Petra said over her shoulder, 'None for me, thanks.'

'Two breakfasts, please,' he repeated, replacing the receiver.

She went to the door, her colour high.

'Where are you going, Miss Bain?'

'For a walk, Mr. Stoddart. I need some fresh, clean air in my lungs.'

He looked at his watch. 'Would you please be back in ten minutes?' It was not a request, it was an order.

Petra thought as she ran down the stairs – the need to run was strangely urgent – come what may, she had to get away from the man. He was overpowering and impossible. She lingered in the forecourt and involuntarily her eyes lifted and she saw him at the bedroom window watching her. Even now, when she had put herself out of his reach, he was dangling her on the end of a line, but she would struggle and twist and free herself from his hook. If she ever let him 'catch' her, he would, when he had no more use for her, throw her back into the water as he had all the other unfortunate women with whom his life had become briefly entangled. Petra Bain, she told herself, would slip from his fingers, uncaught, unscathed.

As she wandered in the rose garden, she remembered the time limit he had set, and those ten minutes had passed. She walked on doggedly, only to pause and remember the original reason for her journey and her ultimate destination, Jay's home, Alaric's home, Underlings.

Alaric looked at his watch as she opened the door. 'Five minutes late.'

He had changed and in his dark suit and sober tie he looked every inch the businessman, the master of the house he apparently ran so efficiently on his absent father's behalf. Every inch, too, the formidable employer, the man wielding the power, giving the orders and – as he had just demonstrated – expecting them to be carried out.

'Breakfast,' he nodded to the table covered with choice foods, cups, plates and a pot of steaming coffee, 'for two. Please sit down.'

Again, it was not so much an invitation as an instruction. She thought it wise, in the circumstances, to obey. As she started eating she discovered she was hungry. It had been hours since she had had any food.

'Who,' he asked, with a slight smile, as she drank her second cup of coffee, 'refused breakfast when I ordered it?'

'I'm sorry, I was wrong, you were right.' Did that please the man? Was she striking the right note, the correct employer-employee relationship?

'I usually am right, Miss Bain.' It was a statement, not a boast. They were the words of a successful executive, with his wits permanently about him, never off guard, never deceived. He watched as she pushed her cup away. 'Had enough?'

She assured him she had. He rang for service and in the lull that followed he wandered to the window. Petra wished he would talk, wondered what he was thinking, picked up a magazine and made an attempt to take in the contents.

The breakfast dishes were cleared, the room was still. Her companion had not moved. At last he said, 'I mentioned earlier that I should like to talk to you.' He turned and rested his back against the windowsill.

She closed the magazine, put it aside and said, 'Yes, Mr. Stoddart.' She crossed her legs, clasped her hands and waited, as she had done so many times in the past while waiting for each employer of the week to take her measure, assess the extent of her intelligence and decide which kind of work could be entrusted to her.

Alaric Stoddart, watching, seemed oddly, but only momentarily, at a loss. 'Are you putting on an act? This is real life, you know, not the dream-like world of the stage.'

'I'm sorry, I don't understand.'

'Nor, frankly, do I.' He pushed his hands into his

trouser pockets, his impeccably tailored jacket draping over them. 'Tell me something. What is your exact position in the Stoddart household going to be?'

Her heart began to beat uncomfortably fast. 'But, Mr. Stoddart, I thought you knew.'

'If I did, I wouldn't be asking.' Another reprimand, but did he have to be so brusque? 'I have the problem of deciding where to install you for the extent of your stay, so it's important that I know. You could, for instance, be coming as Jay's wife-to-be, in which case you would have to be given rooms that fitted your status. You could be his mistress,' involuntarily she drew back at the word, 'in which case, let's not be hypocritical about it, I should have to make a room available to you within easy reach of his. You could be coming to us as his "resting" colleague, in need of a temporary home, rent-free. You would in that case be given a different room again. You could be on holiday and would perhaps have to be pampered a little. You see, there are so many possibilities. You might simply be a hopeful hanger-on, with Jay in your marital sights. You've told me your opinion of him, how much you like him. You might well be in love with my brother. Are you?'

Now she had been given the chance of speaking up for herself, she could find nothing to say. 'If so,' he went on, 'judging by the way he spoke of you last night, and the way he kissed you goodbye, it would seem he might well return your affection. But with what intent, I haven't been able to determine. He's never brought a girl home before, which must surely mean something. But I feel I must warn you, Miss Bain, he has little money.'

The innuendo in his last words had her on the defensive. 'As he told you, Mr. Stoddart,' her voice was surprisingly steady, 'I know only too well how little money he has. He's been able to find a bit more work than I have, as he's more skilled in technical matters, but even that's come to an end.' She went on after a short, thoughtful silence, ' "Money and marriage" you said last night was all a woman, any woman, wanted.'

'I'm sorry you heard. I thought you were too

41

dazed—'

'Or drunk.'

'*Touché.* Or drunk, to hear.'

'Well, I was neither. May I state here and now that the only money I'm interested in is what I shall earn by my own efforts, for my needs and no more.' She hesitated, but plunged on because she felt it was only right to be honest with him. 'You probably won't like what I'm going to say, but,' her eyes held his, 'it's a belief of mine that for any one person to have an excess of wealth and possessions is wrong, morally wrong.' She gazed at him anxiously, trying to gauge his reaction and saw his eyebrows rise slowly and sardonically. He seemed more amused than annoyed, so she took heart and went on, 'And marriage – well, you're wrong again in my case. It doesn't come into my scheme of things. I have a career, a profession to follow.'

'A profession that doesn't seem to want you. And one at which, you admit yourself, you're not outstanding.'

She shrugged hopelessly. 'Given a chance I'd improve, I'm sure I would.'

'All right, so marriage and, you allege, money, is out.' His eyes half-closed. 'You know, you can protest to the contrary as much as you like, but you're an incredibly good actress. I'm convinced you're not half as innocent as you manage to look. What exactly is it you're after, Miss Bain?'

'But, Mr. Stoddart,' her eyes sought his, 'I thought you knew. I thought Jay had told you.' He looked puzzled. 'I'm coming to work for you.'

'For *me*? You intrigue me. Am I permitted to ask in what capacity?' He considered her indolently, then walked over to the bed and turned his eyes on that. 'Don't tell me,' he baited, 'let me guess. And if I guess right, what better place than here and now? You played coy earlier, when I gave you every encouragement, but never mind, perhaps that was just to whet my appetite.' He loosened his tie and started undoing the buttons on his shirt. Then he paused. 'Perhaps I should warn you, I already have a girl-friend, but don't let that worry you.

Through the ages the Stoddarts have been renowned for their virility.'

She stood, her face flaming. She felt for one mad moment that she would like to take his tie between her fingers and pull it until he choked. 'Will you stop insulting me? Will you stop being so – so offensive? And will you please, *please* listen?'

He looked at her keenly and his manner altered. He buttoned his shirt, re-tied his tie and pulled out a chair for her. He sat at one of the writing tables, crossed his legs, folded his arms and waited.

'At last,' she thought, 'the interview I've been waiting for.' And, she reluctantly had to admit, dreading.

CHAPTER THREE

I⊤ was Jay's idea,' Petra began, playing with the ring which was still on her engagement finger.

She was so long in continuing he prompted, 'What was?'

'That I should become a guide.' He said nothing and she dared not meet his eyes. 'His job was coming to an end and he knew I hated the temporary secretarial work I had taken on. He was going home, he said, because the season for tourists was about to start and he would earn some money doing what he and his sister usually did, act as guides to the visitors. He told me I could come, too, and pay my way by doing the same work.

'But how much do you know about the house, the family and its history?'

'Quite a lot, Mr. Stoddart. Jay gave me the booklets you sell to visitors and a pile of typed notes, and I've studied them. Now I know the past history of Underlings and its owners, the Stoddarts, almost better than I know my own.'

'But, Miss Bain,' Alaric said quietly, almost gently, 'there's no vacancy for a guide.'

She looked at him a little wildly. 'Jay said there was. He said you'd be glad to have me there . . .'

'He meant *he* would be glad to have you there.'

'No,' she shook her head until her hair lifted and fell, 'he really meant there would be work for me, money I could earn . . .' The truth sank in. 'So there's no job, no money—' He shook his head. She bit her lip, hiding her face so that he could not see her deep disappointment. Much more and she'd be crying, and that would never do, in front of this man.

She stood up, looking vaguely round for her bag, her case. 'I might as well go home.'

'Where is "home", Miss Bain?' He spoke softly.

Still avoiding his eyes, she shrugged. 'I'll have to find somewhere. I gave up my digs. I didn't think I'd need a place of my own until the autumn, which is when Jay said the visiting season at Underlings was over.' She picked up her handbag. 'In any case I'll have to find somewhere in London. That's where the best agents are, and the acting jobs, if any.'

'Couldn't you go to your parents?'

'No use. They live in a small village outside Durham. My father's a mining engineer. He and my mother live in a cottage. It's hardly big enough for them, let alone me as well.' She picked up her case and went towards the door.

Alaric followed her. 'I might be able to find something for you.' She stopped. 'Jay got you here on false pretences. I owe you something, if only for giving up your digs and getting hit on the head as a result.'

She smiled faintly, but said, 'You owe me nothing, Mr. Stoddart. If anything, it's I who owe you something – for this,' with her head she indicated the hotel room, 'and for feeding me.'

He took her case and put it beside his. 'Sit down again and we'll talk.' Slowly, and because she had little alternative – she doubted if she had enough money to get her back to London – she complied.

'I'll explain the position. The guides are local people. Every spring, summer and early autumn, which is when the house is open to the public, they come to us daily. They're good, trustworthy and knowledgeable, some of them old enough to know my grandparents. They have to be trustworthy. You do understand?'

'Because of the valuables?' Alaric nodded. 'And of course, you don't know me, never met me before last night. It's only natural that you don't trust me . . .'

'I trust you.' She gave him a swift, unbelieving look of gratitude. 'The truth, as I said, is simply that, with Jay and Jenny at home, there's no vacancy. But we run a tea room, self-service, with girls behind the counter. We need help there. Would you be willing to pour tea, make sand-wiches, serve cakes, wash up, clear tables, and after clos-

45

ing time, scrub them spotless?'

Hope shone out of her eyes. 'You're really offering me a job?'

'It wouldn't be beneath your dignity?'

'Out-of-work actors, out-of-work anybody can't afford to have dignity. When you have no money, when you feel the emptiness of your pockets each time your hand goes into them for cash that simply isn't there . . .'

'So you'll take it?'

'Yes, please.'

Their hands met. 'It's a deal,' Alaric said.

The last seventy miles were covered at speed. Petra hoped that Jay wouldn't be far behind. She found herself looking forward to his reappearance with an eagerness that surprised her. He would be the crash barrier between herself and this intimidating man. Whenever Alaric Stoddart came bearing down upon her, she could take cover behind his younger brother. But it occurred to her, in her subordinate, rather humble position as a kitchen hand – that was what she was going to be, wasn't it? – she probably wouldn't see much of the master of Underlings, any more than employees saw much of the managing director of a firm.

Her thoughts on the subject were confirmed by his next words. 'You realize we have a great number of staff, domestic, clerical, administrative? We have gardeners, we have cleaning staff who are skilled in the maintenance of the priceless objects passed down the centuries. We employ people specially trained in the repair of tapestries, seat covers, curtain materials. I suppose you also appreciate that the resident staff at Underlings are divided into different categories and live their own separate lives?'

'You mean,' she said, her training as an actress helping her to keep her voice even, 'that I wouldn't be treated as one of the family?' He inclined his head. 'That I'd have to live in the servants' quarters, mix with them outside working hours, and never, never set foot on the sacred floor of the great house itself?' He smiled. 'And that, if I

46

entertained my boy-friend, Jay Stoddart, son of the owner, I should have to do so on my own territory, amongst my own kind?' He smiled again, but said nothing. She went on, as if to herself, 'The present heir to Underlings is determined not to let history repeat itself, not to allow his father to leave the mansion and the estate to the servants, the subordinates, the underlings.'

'Aren't you over-stating the case a little? And aren't you going back on what you said earlier at the hotel – that someone in your position couldn't afford to have "dignity". Does it hurt your pride to have to mix with the so-called "lower orders"?'

'Of course it doesn't!'

'You sound angry.' He glanced at her flushed face. 'You look angry.'

She said, breathing hard, 'No, I'm not!' He laughed then, as if he were enjoying the situation. He looked at her hands which were gripping her handbag.

'I see you're still "engaged" to me.'

Colour flooded her cheeks as she moved the ring back to her right hand. 'I'm sorry, I forgot.'

'It wasn't a Freudian slip of the memory, was it?'

'No, it was not!'

'So you'd never take on the role of mistress of Underlings, even if you were offered it? But think of the rewards, the honour attached to the "part".'

'They wouldn't interest me. I'd never marry a man simply to acquire status and a fortune. And I'd never marry a man who didn't love me.'

'Not even if you loved him?'

'If I were ever unfortunate enough to fall in love with a man who didn't return my love, I'd keep it to myself. I'd never let him know. In fact, I'd remove myself as far away from him as I possibly could.'

Petra lowered her head against the head-rest attached to the seat. The bump over her temple was still in evidence and throbbed now and then. She closed her eyes and felt sleep closing down like a safety curtain blotting out the stage. The short, uncomfortable night was catching up with her.

'Miss Bain.' A hand rested on her arm. 'We're nearly home.'

'Home', he'd said. His, not hers. 'I'm sorry.' She sat stiffly. 'I didn't realize how tired I was.'

Alaric moved his head towards the window. 'Underlings.'

She held her breath, unable for a moment to release it. Far below the road they were on, looking small because of the distance, but as the car approached growing rapidly larger was a vast, turreted and gabled building, its dazzling whiteness standing out against the rich woodlands and lawns in which it was set. Roads led to the great mansion from all directions. As they drew nearer, Petra saw other buildings joined on to the main. Clustering round, as if afraid of being forgotten, were shrubs, rhododendron bushes, and young cypress trees.

'Your home?' she whispered. 'It's beautiful beyond words.'

'And,' he taunted, smiling, 'do you still think it immoral of me to live in a place so grand, for such a place to have been passed down the centuries for my father to own, and for his family to occupy, exclusive of all others?'

'Such a place,' she answered undaunted, 'should belong to the nation. It shouldn't be privately owned.' She tore her eyes away and looked at him. 'It should belong to the National Trust, they would hold it and maintain it for the ordinary people of the country.'

'Thanks for the advice, which was not asked for,' he said curtly, 'but this is my *home*. Would your parents give *their* home in its entirety to someone else, the home they love?'

The car swept into the grounds and began the long drive towards the house. They were still some way from it and they drove in silence. She felt an odd need to apologize, to counteract the hostility she had aroused in him.

'I'm sorry,' she said, 'to have views so diametrically opposed to yours.' He said nothing. 'I can't help it, Mr. Stoddart. It's probably because of the difference in our backgrounds.' The silence stretched between them. 'It's just as well,' she murmured, 'that I'm going to live in the servants' quarters, isn't it? The fact that we think so differently won't matter, will it, because we won't come into contact with each other.'

His profile was hard and told her nothing. She had probably stepped out of line again. In her dealings with him – if she had any before she left his service – she would probably be doing it constantly.

The car, large though it was, was dwarfed by the house. As it sighed to a stop in front of the pillars and steps which led to the main entrance, a man whom Petra guessed to be the chauffeur came from the shadows. He must have watched the car's progress along the drive. Before the man reached the driver's door, Alaric had got out, so the chauffeur helped Petra to her feet.

Petra thanked him and he nodded and smiled deferentially. 'When he knows,' she thought ruefully, 'that I'm no higher than he is in the domestic servants' hierarchy, perhaps considerably lower, he'll treat me very differently.'

'Bring the cases into the hall, Holmer,' Alaric directed. 'Then put the car away, will you?'

The man touched his cap and went round to the boot of the car.

'Come this way, Miss Bain.' Alaric led the way into the house.

A middle-aged woman, white-haired and pink-cheeked, was coming down the wide, red-carpeted staircase which ended with a flourish of carving in the great, echoing entrance hall. She welcomed the owner's son with a smile.

'Good to see you back, **Mr. Stoddart**,' she said. 'Did **you enjoy** your trip? And **Lady Yvette**, was she well?'

'Yes to your first question,' was the answer, 'and to your second, when I left the young lady in question late last night, she was in excellent health but bad humour.' He flicked a glance at Petra. 'I had to leave her in rather a hurry.' He introduced Petra. 'A colleague of my brother's.

49

Miss Bain, this is the family's own housekeeper, Mrs. Osborn.'

The housekeeper said, with a smile, 'May I ask, Miss Bain, if that means you're in the acting profession like Mr. Jay?'

Petra looked uncertainly at Alaric, who was jingling the money in his pocket with some impatience.

'Well, I—' said Petra, 'I suppose the answer's yes, whenever I can persuade a producer to give me a part in a play!'

'Let's say she's wandering around on the perimeter of it at present, Mrs. Osborn.' The housekeeper laughed. 'Miss Bain had an unfortunate bang on the head last night as a result of my brother's erratic driving. There was an accident.' Mrs. Osborn looked concerned. 'My brother escaped injury – amazing how good luck always seems to go with him – but my brother's passenger did not. He had to stay with the car, which took the brunt of the crash, but he should be along some time today.'

'How is your head, Miss Bain?' the housekeeper said. 'Would you like a doctor to have a look at her, Mr. Stoddart?'

'It might be a good idea. Call Dr. Spicer.'

'No, thank you, Mr. Stoddart,' Petra said hastily. 'There's really no need.'

Alaric lifted his hand and put his fingers gently on the bump. 'Does that hurt?'

She winced. 'A little, but it's gone down, surely you can feel it has?'

He looked into her face. 'You look pale.'

She covered her cheeks as if to hide them from him. 'I'm always pale.'

'Anaemic, probably, lack of nourishing food.' His smile held a touch of malice. 'Which is the greater evil, Miss Bain, too much money, or too little?'

His words brought a tinge of colour to her cheeks. She answered steadily, 'The former, Mr. Stoddart. By having barely enough to live on, at least I'm hurting no one but myself, whereas if someone has too much—'

'I get the implication, Miss Bain. I know your views.

You've expounded them clearly enough already. Mrs. Osborn.' The housekeeper, who had been listening with deep interest, responded with a questioning smile. 'Miss Bain and I will lunch together. If my brother arrives in time, he can join us. Where's my sister?'

Mrs. Osborn looked a little embarrassed. 'Somewhere in the grounds, Mr. Stoddart. I doubt if she'll be in for lunch. She asked the cook to make up some sandwiches. Said it was such a nice day she'd have a picnic with – she'd have a picnic.'

'Yes, I can guess with whom.' He motioned to Petra to go with him up the stairs and he muttered, 'The girl's throwing herself at him.'

'Mr. Stoddart?' Alaric turned and looked down at the housekeeper. 'Where are Miss Bain's cases to go?'

He began to speak, changed his mind, looked at Petra and asked, 'You want to change before lunch?'

Shyly she shook her head. 'Only wash, if I may.'

'Leave them in the hall for the moment, Mrs. Osborn.'

With a 'Yes, Mr. Stoddart' she bustled away. Alaric walked through an archway at the top of the staircase, moving so quickly Petra had no time to appreciate the beauty all round her. Instead there was a vague residual blur left in her mind, like the rainbow flash in the wake of a passing kingfisher.

They turned a corner at the end of a long corridor, coming to a stop in front of a large brown-varnished door marked 'Private'. Her host turned the handle and stood back to allow her to pass in front of him. 'These are the family's living quarters. No member of the public is allowed beyond this door.'

Halfway along another corridor, he turned and sprinted up a flight of stairs. 'These are the bedrooms.' As they passed by, Petra lost count of the doors, there were so many. In a small alcove were three white doors clustered together. 'One of the bathrooms, shower-room and so on. I have my own bedroom suite, which includes a bathroom. Jay and Jenny have their own rooms, too. My father's suite is kept always ready in case he comes home unexpectedly. It's a rare event. The main guest room is likewise kept permanently available. When you've finished, would you return along this corridor, go down the stairs and I'll be there to take you to the dining-room for lunch.'

She thanked him and he left her without a smile. Petra was so anxious not to keep her illustrious host waiting she arrived too soon at the appointed meeting place. He was not there.

She walked up and down the corridor and as the moments passed her agitation increased. What would she say to him over dinner, what would they talk about? She wanted to run away and join Mrs. Osborn who looked so motherly and considerate, so kindly and understanding, all the things she needed to boost her courage as she waited, like a nervous small-part player for her cue to go onstage.

There were footsteps, but were they going up or down? Like a thief caught in the act her head turned first one way then the other.

'Petra?' The voice came from behind and she swung round. Jay appeared at the top of a flight of stairs hidden from view. She ran to meet him and his arms opened wide. Within them was the kindliness and understanding she could not, because of protocol, beg for from Mrs. Osborn. Here was escape from the man who frightened her and who filled her with a terrible sense of inadequacy as no other man had ever done before.

'Jay,' she whispered, 'oh, Jay, it's good to see you again!'

'Such a welcome!' said Jay, nuzzling her ear. 'Like a favourite dog barking with joy and wagging his tail fit to shake it off.'

She laughed, with relief as much as with amusement. 'How did you get here?'

'Hired a car. How badly were you hurt, sweetie?'

'Just a bump. It's going down.'

'Then what's the matter? There's something wrong. What happened after I left you?'

'We drove on, slept a bit,' she passed over the rest, 'then

this morning we called at a fabulous hotel.' She smiled. 'A new experience for me. We had breakfast. Came on here.'

Jay pulled her close. 'He didn't touch you?'

'Your brother?' She frowned. Alaric Stoddart had had no need to 'touch' her. She had 'felt' him, the impact, the pulling power, the dangerous attraction, like the edge of a precipice drawing a climber against his will. 'No, he didn't touch me.'

'She's right, boy. I didn't "touch" her.' Petra pulled herself from Jay's arms and turned angrily to meet Alaric's sardonic smile. How long had he been standing there?

'She only slept in my arms in the back of the car.' He watched for his brother's reaction and saw it with satisfaction.

'Petra?' Jay asked. 'Is that true?'

Petra turned away.

'Don't panic,' said Alaric. 'We didn't put the springs of the back seat to the test as you would have done had she travelled all the way in yours.'

'Keep your hands off her, Alaric. You can do what you like with your own woman, but leave mine alone!'

'So she's your "woman", is she?' Alaric looked her over insultingly. 'I thought as much, despite her "touch me not" act this morning at the hotel.'

Jay's lips tightened. 'So you tried it on? I guessed you might.'

Petra thought, two brothers quarrelling over me? For heaven's sake, why? A family argument was the last thing she could stand. 'Jay, Mr. Stoddart, please . . . I'm desperately tired. May I sit down?'

Alaric opened a door. 'This way, Miss Bain.'

The private dining-room had more of the touch of homeliness about it than the main part of the house. The wallpaper was a delicate pink with an elaborate embossed pattern. The furniture was light oak, the carpet woven in muted colours.

But even in the family's living quarters, away from the public gaze, it was impossible to forget the Stoddart ancestry. Paintings gazed down, some of them of great personages of the past, but mostly of those living today. Over the small white fireplace was the largest portrait in a carved, gold-painted frame.

Alaric, watching Petra, said carelessly, 'My father.' He was bearded, dark-haired, with an expression which Petra had caught once or twice on his elder son's face – a little hard, a little sardonic but, unlike his son, with an affability and warmth which reached out and touched the onlooker.

To the left was another, newer portrait – Alaric Stoddart, dark-eyed, black-haired, inscrutable, painted perhaps four or five years before, his elbow resting languidly on a mantelshelf. Even his portrait held a magnetism which Petra found fascinating and irresistible. Nearby was a painting of Jay and, presumably, his twin sister Jenny, painted, it seemed, when they were in their late teens.

'My mother, some years before she died.' Alaric indicated the picture of a woman in a pale yellow, simply-cut evening gown, her brown hair caught back, her mouth softened by a faint smile. There was Jay in her, and presumably Jenny, but not a trace of her first child. Alaric was his father's son, no doubt about it.

'Sit down, Petra.' Jay waved towards the table laid with woven place-mats, gleaming silver cutlery, white table napkins and bowls of flowers. But Petra, uncertain of what was expected of her, looked towards his brother, as if for permission. Alaric pulled out a chair for her at the centre of one side. Jay took his place opposite her and Alaric sat at the head.

It seemed right that he should sit there. The only thing that was missing was a woman, the mistress of the house, at the other end. No doubt his beautiful, high-born lady friend occupied that seat when she was visiting her loved one.

As soon as they were seated, the door was pushed open and a maid served the meal. Petra smiled at the girl who seemed too shy to smile back. 'Just wait,' thought Petra, 'until she sees me at my new job behind the counter in the tea room. She won't be shy of me then.'

The two men discussed the fate of Jay's car. 'The garage can patch it up,' said Jay. 'It'll be ready in a week. I said I'd go and fetch it.' He drank a spoonful of soup and glanced tentatively at his brother. 'They would have delivered it, but I couldn't afford to let them do it, plus the charge for the repairs.' Alaric seemed preoccupied with his lunch. Jay sighed. 'Pity. It's a long way to go.'

'Can't I help, Jay?' Petra offered, touched, as she usually was, by the indignity of a man without money, especially Jay. 'I've put some savings aside from what I've earned typing. If it's any help, you can have it . . .'

'*You* help?' The question from Alaric was edged with something curiously like anger. 'It's hardly your problem, if I may say so.'

'It is, Mr. Stoddart,' Petra said. 'Jay and I share our problems.'

'And our money,' Jay added. 'When she's in need—'

'Which is pretty often,' Petra broke in.

'—I help, and when I'm in need, likewise, she helps. We out-of-work types stick together.' Jay pushed away his plate. 'You don't know how the other half lives, Alaric. *You* should try living on coffee and a ham sandwich and find yourself looking on a two-course meal as a luxury, like us. Go on, call it gross mismanagement of funds, with your usual brotherly delicacy.'

'I don't see how,' Petra said, glancing at her future employer, 'anyone can call struggling to live on practically nothing "gross mismanagement".'

Now Alaric pushed away his plate as if he could not stand the sight of it. 'Look, Miss Bain, before we proceed any further in our relationship, let's get this clear. If Jay is forced down to the level of living on "practically nothing", it's *his* fault, not mine. Education-wise, he was offered all the chances I was given. I went to all the best schools, so did Jay. There the similarity ends. To put it simply, I worked hard because I wanted to. Jay did not work hard because he did not want to. I went to university – by my own efforts. Again by my own efforts I attained a first-class honours degree. Jay could have done

55

likewise had he chosen to do so. Poor as his academic achievements were at school, he could have been coached to the required standard. He chose instead, although warned against it by our many contacts in the theatre, to by-pass university education and opted for drama school. He disregarded all warnings that the theatre was a rat race, the competition soul-destroying, the monetary return in the lower reaches of the theatrical world scant.'

Jay fiddled uncomfortably with the cutlery, saying nothing in his own defence.

Alaric went on, 'If he's now impoverished you can hardly expect me to weep on his behalf. Nor can you expect me constantly to put my hand in my pocket for him. The money I earn as manager of this house and estate comes to me through sheer hard work, not inheritance. The financial returns from my directorships do not come to me by waving a wand, but again by working for them. Having got that straight, I should be obliged if you would stop regarding me as the devil incarnate where my brother and sister are concerned. They chose their lives. I chose mine. Is that clear?'

Miserably, Petra nodded.

'Look, Alaric,' Jay began, but the maid came in with the main course. When she had gone, Alaric said shortly,

'Have the car delivered. Send the bill to me.'

Jay stared. 'You mean the bill for delivery?'

'And the repairs. The lot.' He looked sarcastically at Petra. 'Now perhaps in Miss Bain's eyes I might start to grow wings instead of horns.'

'That's good of you, Alaric,' said Jay. 'I appreciate that.'

'And what about you, Miss Bain?' The dark eyes narrowed. 'Do *you* think it's good of me? Do you applaud my "Robin Hood" act? You approve of one of the "rich" giving away some of his money to the "poor and needy"?'

Petra looked at him, but looked away at once. She could not hold those glinting eyes for long. 'Very much,

Mr. Stoddart.'

Jay said, his appetite partially appeased, his pleasure at his brother's unexpectedly benevolent gesture making him expansive and flushed as if he had over-indulged in drink, 'What's all this "Miss Bain", "Mr. Stoddart" nonsense? We can't have this formality amongst friends and family. Call him Alaric, sweetie. That's his name.' He reached across the table and took her hand. 'You don't call *me* Mr. Stoddart, do you?' He looked at his brother. 'Any more than I call your woman Lady Yvette. If your girl's Yvette to me, why isn't my girl Petra to you?'

There was a pause, then, sharply, 'Well, Miss Bain, what's the answer?'

Petra turned to Alaric. 'As far as I am concerned, Mr. Stoddart, you can call me what you like. I shall continue to call you Mr. Stoddart. I've come here as neither friend nor family,' with a smile, 'sorry, Jay, I've come here to work. And,' she fiddled with her glass of water, 'a kitchen hand can hardly call her employer by his first name, can she? After all, what would the girls who will be working with me think?'

'Hey,' Jay looked at his brother, 'what's all this about a kitchen hand? I brought her here to act as a guide.'

'So she told me. Since when have you been in a position to offer people jobs on my behalf and without even consulting me? I happen to be in charge. Instead of taking so much for granted, wouldn't it have been better to have phoned me first, before making your offer?'

'But we always need guides. Old man Winters is on his last legs. It's time he was given the push.'

'And what would our enthusiastic supporter of people's rights,' he looked narrowly at Petra, 'think of Alaric the Second, as she apparently calls me, if I were to fire an old man – and one who knew my grandfather – from a position he's held and loved for many years, simply because, as you put it, he's on his last legs? And because his job was wanted to accommodate Miss Petra Bain, a newcomer with no connections with the area, the local people or the house? And whose only reason for being here is that she's an out-of-work actress and happens also to be your girl-friend? What would you say, Miss Bain?'

Miss Bain was forced into silence. Whatever she said would be wrong, she thought. If she agreed with Jay she would be going against her own principles – and giving her future employer a stick to beat her with. If she agreed with Alaric she would hurt Jay, who had only had her own good in mind when he had invited her there.

'Miss Bain and I discussed the position this morning,' Alaric went on. 'When I told her there was no vacancy for a guide, she was disappointed, but understood. So I offered her a job in the tea room. She accepted. Confirm that, Miss Bain. I can see the hurt expression on your loved one's face. I doubt if he believes me. He probably thinks I forced the job on you. He's also no doubt convinced that I forced myself on you.' She looked at him, remembering, and this time their eyes held. 'Did I, Miss Bain?'

Jay saw the exchange of glances. 'There are more ways than one of forcing yourself on a girl, and boy, do you know the lot!'

'It's all right, Jay. Your brother behaved no differently from many other men in similar circumstances.'

'Which isn't saying much,' interposed Jay.

'And I was only too glad to be offered a job – any job – in the tea room. Anyway,' she looked out of the window at the great park in which the house was standing, 'who am I, with my state school education, my humble upbringing in a four-roomed cottage by poverty-haunted parents, to regard myself as being above such work as a kitchen hand?'

'That's right,' Jay grinned, 'give it to him! It's time someone gave old Alaric a verbal punch on the nose!'

'Miss Bain,' came the quiet voice from the head of the table, 'you spoke somewhat unguardedly last night. You may remember that I remarked on it at the time, but I made allowances because I realized you were in a dazed condition. But,' the warning note was unmistakable, 'at this moment you are, I'm sure, completely in command of your own faculties and well aware of what you're saying.

58

I didn't have to offer you any job. When you suggested you would return to London, I could have let you go.'

'He's saying don't bite the hand that's going to feed you, Pet,' Jay said, 'otherwise he'll send you to bed without any tea. Talking of bed,' he looked at his brother, 'which room's she going to have, the one next to mine?'

'She can sleep in the converted stables with the other members of the domestic staff.'

'She can *what*?' He pushed back his chair. 'Petra, did my brother consult you about this?' Slowly and a little sadly, she shook her head. This was totally unexpected. Not only had she been relegated job-wise, but he was putting her socially from him, pushing her bodily out of the family circle.

'I can take it, Jay. I think I understand your brother's train of thought. If I were given a room here, if I were accepted as a friend, what would the other girls think? They wouldn't like me or trust me.'

But Jay would not be pacified. 'If she's put over there, she'll have to share a room with one or even two others. How can I, son of the owner, go over there and see her? Not only would it embarrass them like hell, it would embarrass me. Have a heart, Alaric. She's my girl. How can I touch her and kiss her in front of an audience?'

The answer came dryly, 'Isn't that precisely what you were taught to do at drama school?'

Petra tried to save the situation. 'It's all right, Jay. I'll meet you outside somewhere, in the grounds perhaps – with my employer's permission, of course.' Her eyes looking at Alaric were provoking.

He saw it and was provoked. 'For such activities as you have in mind, Miss Bain, it would not be advisable for you to seek my permission or for me to give it. We might get involved in a tangle with the law. It's happened through the ages – the seduction of kitchen hands, milkmaids, parlourmaids, call them what you will, by the sons of owners of the property. It's happened in the past at Underlings. If any offspring were to result from such a liaison, had I given my "permission" you might, with your insistence on equal rights, make all kinds of claims

59

against me, not to mention my father, such as financial support for yourself and said offspring.'

'Don't be so damned insulting, Alaric!' Jay burst out.

'If Miss Bain consciously challenges me, then she has to learn to take what she asks for.'

Petra thought, the man's a monster after all. How much lower could he push her? But of course, he hated actresses, didn't he? 'Reared up and pawed the air,' Jay had said, at the mention of them.

She thought it advisable to remove herself from his presence with all possible speed. She rose, thanking him for allowing her to have her meal with the family. He looked at her suspiciously, but judged that she had meant it sincerely. He was right. She told herself that she had, after all, forced herself upon him, upon the household. Knowing Jay, she should have asked him if he had sought his brother's permission to bring her, but in her elation at having the chance of a job that promised to be both pleasant and interesting, she forgot to ask questions.

'Where are you going, Miss Bain?'

She frowned. Where was she going? 'I – I don't know, Mr. Stoddart.'

'Then you'd better sit down again, hadn't you?'

She complied.

'There must be somewhere else she can go,' said Jay, walking to the window and back to the table. 'All right, so she can't sleep in the house. But—' he brightened, 'what about the old coach house? You had it repaired and furnished and made into a weekend hideout for Jenny, but she hardly ever uses it. Couldn't you let Petra have that? It's only till the season's over, Alaric.'

Alaric's fingers drummed, his eyes lifted to Petra. 'What about it, Miss Bain? It's only a short distance from the stables, but it stands alone. You would have some privacy.'

Appreciation shone in her eyes. 'It's good of you, Mr. Stoddart. Thanks, Jay.'

He rested his cheek on her hair. 'Anything to please the girl in my life.'

'It's in his interests, isn't it?' said his brother, rising and watching them. 'As the son of the owner, tradition confers on him the right of free and unimpeded access to any of the women domestic workers on the staff.'

Petra flushed and Jay ground his teeth. 'Say that again, brother . . .'

Alaric ignored the challenge. 'I'll allow you the pleasure of showing Miss Bain to her new quarters, Jay. I hope you'll find them comfortable, Miss Bain.'

She regarded him steadily. 'After the digs and the cramped conditions I've been living in over the past few years, Mr. Stoddart, I can assure you that even an old converted coach house will seem like heaven.'

Alaric turned at the door. 'Now that is something I wouldn't know. With all the power I wield and all the wealth you insist I possess, it hasn't – yet – been my good fortune to encounter heaven on earth. I may have come near to it, but it stays just outside my reach. It seems to be something money just can't buy.'

CHAPTER FOUR

The building might once have been a coach house, but with the taste and money that had been lavished on it, it had taken on the air of a rich man's country cottage. It was stone-built with a red-tiled roof and small, square windows. Climbing flowers had been trained to grow round the low beamed front door. Inside, carpets covered the varnished floor boards, the furniture was second-hand but of sound quality, the fabric of the curtains and wing chair chosen with a consciousness of the surroundings they would be called upon to enhance.

The fireplace, although a recent addition, was wide and welcoming and constructed in deep red brick. At the top of a short flight of stairs was a bedroom with a shallow sloping roof. The small casement window opened to overlook the cobbled yard and Petra could see the converted stables in which a number of the domestic staff were housed.

Petra spent the afternoon unpacking and getting the feel of the place. A man came to light the fire, leaving a pile of logs and a supply of coal. A girl came with clean, aired sheets and blankets and made the bed. A young boy brought an electric convector heater for the bedroom.

That there was someone directing operations Petra had no doubt. It couldn't be Jay, because he was too much in the clouds to think of the simple necessities of life. It was probably not the housekeeper, either. She would hardly have the necessary authority. It was almost certainly Alaric Stoddart himself who was the mind behind it all, issuing orders not out of any consideration for her, but because it was his job to look after the physical well-being of his staff.

Petra wandered to the bedroom window. She opened it and leaned on the sill. Just above her head in the eaves, birds were squabbling. There seemed to be a nest there with young birds in it. They were at home, she reflected, in their own surroundings not in an alien, unfriendly environment like her.

Her eyes scanned the parkland, the fields and woods which spread, rich and abundant, into the far distance. She envied Jay his heritage. Even if he never managed to get an acting job again, he would have this solidity behind him, this home of his to go back to, while she had – what? A cottage in a mining village for a home and as an occupation shorthand-typing, moving from one claustrophobic office to another.

She noticed two figures walking slowly towards the house, a girl's and a young man's. As they approached, Petra caught the sound of voices which were raised, it seemed in argument. The young man started to turn away, but the girl caught his arm. He tried to free himself, but she clasped her arms round his neck and kissed him. At first he resisted, but, as if he couldn't help himself, he started to return her kiss. Then he pushed her away and walked off without once looking back.

The girl continued walking towards the house, her figure disconsolate, her feet trailing. She was dressed in a check blouse tucked into blue jeans and a carrier bag swung from her fingers. Abstractedly her eyes lifted to contemplate the coach house. She saw Petra and stood still. The girl, with her colouring, her bright, open face, was so like Jay that if it had not been for her long brown hair she could almost have been mistaken for him.

'Hi, there,' she called. 'Who's been sleeping in *my* bed?' She ran to the coach house and met Petra at the bottom of the stairs. Her hand came out. 'Goldilocks?' she asked, laughing. 'Because if you are, I'm an absolutely *furious* Baby Bear!'

Petra laughed. 'You're Jenny, Jay's twin?'

'None other! And you? You're not,' she paused, 'you're not Alaric's latest?'

Did her elder brother have such a reputation? Petra shook her head. 'A friend of Jay's.'

'So, it goes without saying, a friend of mine. Welcome to Underlings. What's your name?' Petra told her. 'You wouldn't, by any chance, be an actress?'

'Sorry,' said Petra, 'in theory, yes. In practice, I'm "resting".'

'Why the apology? Ah, I can guess – my big brother. How did the boss take that little piece of information? I bet he turned his venom on you as only he can! And you've infiltrated this far into the Stoddart household? After an encounter with his lordship, being an actress it's a wonder you escaped with your life!'

'I don't think he likes me very much,' Petra said slowly.

Jenny laughed. 'That's probably an understatement! What are you doing here, on holiday or,' her eyes sought Petra's left hand, 'meeting the family?'

'Neither. Believe it or not, I'm coming to be an Underlings' underling.' Jenny frowned. 'I'm going to work for Mr. Stoddart.'

'Alaric? In what capacity?' When she heard, Petra thought, would her friendly manner melt away? Would she become – and as the owner's daughter she would be entitled to become – withdrawn, cool and dismissing? 'And,' Jenny went on, 'what's all this "Mr. Stoddart" business? He's Alaric to all our friends. Why not you?'

'Shall we sit down?' Petra asked. 'If I'm allowed to invite you to sit down in your own place!' They sat on the wing chairs while Petra told her story.

'So he's not allowing you to be a guide? He's put you in the tea room as though you hadn't the intelligence to do anything else? I'll tell Big Brother just what I think of him!'

So the girl had remained Jay's twin sister, after all, warm and outgoing, as unspoilt by her background as Jay himself. Petra experienced a rush of thankfulness that here she had found another ally in the desert of unfriendliness that she had so far found Underlings to be.

Jenny went into the tiny kitchen and made them both a cup of tea. She showed Petra where the food was kept, the crockery and other necessities. 'I'll say this for dear Alaric, he has his moments. He poured a lot of money into the rebuilding of this place. He can be surprisingly generous when he wants. I got this house out of him by catching him in a good mood – a rare event! But there's something he is mean about and that's affection, sympathy and so on. How he treats his woman I dare not think. But she clings all the same. You know he's got a girl-friend? If one can apply such a lowly expression to the Lady Yvette. Jay and I hate her. Every time she comes, we do our best to freeze her out, but her protective covering's so thick, it makes no impression. She regards us as a couple of nuisances and if she dared I think she'd tell us to run away and play!'

As they washed the cups, Jenny frowned and said, concentrating on swilling the washing-up bowl, 'Did you witness that touching little scene while you were looking out of the bedroom window? His name's Martyn Parker. I admit it's a blatant case of "woman chases man", the reason being that Martyn regards me not only as royalty – you know, he, an underprivileged "commoner", could never rise to my social level and ask me to marry him – but he disapproved of the whole set-up. It's not only politics, with him it's sheer, blind prejudice.' Jenny looked round and Petra saw how deeply she felt the rejection of the man she obviously loved. 'He's got this thing about social equality. He says Underlings and all the other stately homes should be pulled down, that they're nothing but anachronisms, museums, and so on.'

'Does he work here?' Petra asked.

Jenny nodded. 'In the conservatory, growing rare plants. He's a horticulturalist. He's got a degree in the subject. He says he came here for the experience, and when he's got that, you won't see him for dust.' Her voice trembled. 'Which leaves Jennifer Stoddart right out in the cold.' She dried her hands. 'I keep telling him my father gives me an allowance. With what he earns, we could live quite well on that. But as he delights in saying, the Stoddart set-up goes against the grain as well as his principles and he just won't listen.'

She shook her shoulders and threw off her gloom. 'But one day I'll make him listen. If he goes away, I'll just follow him. Alaric can have his precious stately home and the title that goes with it. Not to mention the beautiful

Yvette who'll share it with him one day. Have you seen the house yet? Artistically speaking, it's beyond description. I suppose a little bit of me is proud of it, and I think it's the same with Jay.' Which, Petra thought, is just what I've been telling myself, isn't it?

'Come on, Petra, I'll do the honours. I'll rehearse my piece, get back into practice before the hordes descend. You know the season begins the day after tomorrow?' She recited monotonously, as if she had said it many times before, 'From Easter to the end of September, Tuesdays to Saturdays eleven to six and Sunday afternoons, not to mention Mondays at Easter and the various Bank Holidays. Lunches and teas are served in the Barn Tearoom.'

'Are you there, Pet?' Jay's voice called from the living-room.

'Yes, darling,' Jenny answered in a false, high voice. 'Pet's here.'

'What the—?' Jay asked, standing in the kitchen doorway. 'Oh, it's you, angel face. I might have known. What the blazes are you doing here?' Jay put his arm round Petra. 'Didn't you know three's a crowd? Get out, there's a good girl.'

'You can't turn your sister off her own property. Anyway, I'm taking your Pet round the house. No one's had the good manners to show your guest the darned building yet.'

'We'll both show her. Come on, darling,' to Petra, 'do the infamous Stoddart twins the honour of coming between them.' He threw a log on the fire and sparks rose up the chimney like a firework display.

Jay took one arm and Jenny the other, and they walked Petra along the cobbled yard, past the stables and into the great house through the back door They pulled her between them up the wide, glinting stone staircase into the private wing of the house, rushed her past the bewildering sameness of the multiplicity of doors, turned the handle of the door marked 'Private' and stopped to get their breaths back.

They turned right, and went through the archway

which graced the top of a flight of an even more gracious staircase and, still three abreast, stepped in a more dignified way down the soft red and black carpeting into the entrance hall itself. They lingered in front of the marble statuettes, pointed out the intricate metalwork of the shining brass banister and the balconies high to the right and left of them.

With a sweep of the hand they indicated the magnificent wall paintings by eminent artists of the past, depicting scenes from the lives of various Roman emperors. They took her along a corridor lined with antique furniture, the window bays filled with flowers from the gardens. They made a lightning tour of the Lower Dining Room set for a meal with gold-painted plates and silverware. Around the walls, wherever they went, were portraits, always portraits.

'That's my great-great-grandfather,' Jenny said. 'Look at his fierce expression. I expect that's where Alaric gets it from.'

'There's our four times great-grandmother. She was a beauty in her day,' said Jay. Which, Petra calculated, must have taken them back a couple of centuries. And still the Stoddart look came through.

Into the State Dining Room now, the painted ceilings representing, Jenny explained, one of the ancient Italian schools of artists. The walls, she said, were covered in embossed leather, roughly early eighteenth century. The table was set for a banquet of distant times. There were silver plates and candlesticks and the china, Jay told her, was part of the Sèvres dinner service. The chairs were antique, the glassware sparkling. She was taken into the Saloon, a vast, elaborately decorated room with priceless hanging tapestries, gilded, richly upholstered settees and chairs.

There, over the richly ornamental fireplace, was a painting of Sir Cecil Stoddart, who had disowned his profligate son, Alaric, and left Underlings to his servants. Near him was Alaric the First himself, his devil-may-care character in his handsome face, a challenging expression in his dark, unflinching eyes. This was the present-day

Alaric in embryo, dominating, magnetic yet daunting, with a charm which would be a woman's downfall if, as Petra knew by experience, she had not the strength of will to resist it.

Jay and Jenny took Petra upstairs to the State bedrooms with their rich tapestries, painted ceilings and four-poster beds where kings and queens had slept in times gone by. They strolled along the Dress Corridor which displayed clothes worn by past Stoddarts on ceremonial occasions.

Jenny fingered, with a strange longing, the white satin wedding dress worn by Stoddart brides from her great-grandmother onwards, perhaps knowing that, loving the man she had chosen to love, it would never be hers to wear.

As Petra went from room to room, she felt that, encapsuled in the twin brother and sister beside her, she was in the presence of all the Stoddarts of the past, the present and those to come. In their faces and their voices was a pride they didn't even realize they possessed. They were part of history, it lived in them, and however much they tried to persuade themselves otherwise, Petra knew they would never escape from the out-reaching tentacles of their background and their inheritance.

To ask them and their brother Alaric, to give away any part of this magnificence was like asking them to give up part of themselves. They merged with their ancestors, were one with them because, by glance, expression, or a sudden light in the eye they revealed that their forebears lived on in them. Petra supposed it was true of all peoples, but only in those like Jenny, Jay and Alaric Stoddart, who were lucky enough to have their past here and now, visible, tangible before them, did it become palpable and real.

'Impressed?' asked Jay, putting his arm round Petra and pulled her close. They were back in the private quarters and lingering in the corridor.

Petra nodded. What else could she do? She was breathless with wonder and full of humility, too, for the glories and achievements of the Stoddarts of the past.

'There,' said Jenny, pointing along a short corridor which was an off-shoot of the one they were standing in, 'is the administrative section. Down there is the boss's office, his secretaries, the assistant estate manager, and so on. Sometimes I help Alaric with office work. Why the surprise? Don't I look the secretary type?'

'No,' Jay answered, 'any more than Petra looks the typical, sexy actress type.' He turned her face towards him as a door opened, but he kissed her on the mouth before he let her go. He saw Alaric standing outside his office door. Jay said to his brother, as if he had been addressing him from the start, 'Don't mistake my meaning. I'm not saying Petra hasn't got all a man could want. Don't you agree, Alaric?'

Alaric came towards them and said coldly, 'I haven't had time yet to assess the extent and quality of Miss Bain's sensuality. No doubt the opportunity will arise before long.'

Jay tugged Petra towards him so hard she fell against his side. 'I told you before, Alaric, hands off.'

'Then you shouldn't ask leading questions, should you, brother? What do you three want?'

'Just showing our *guest* round,' said Jenny.

Alaric's eyebrows rose. 'I wasn't aware that she was our guest. I've never known a guest demand a job with a regular weekly wage.'

'What's the matter, Alaric?' Jenny said petulantly. 'Can't you be pleasant to Jay's girl? What harm has she ever done you?' He didn't reply. Jenny took Petra's arm. 'Come on, let's get out from under the ogre's feet. Didn't I tell you he's hardly ever in a good mood?'

He cut across her sisterly remarks with a curt, 'How's your head, Miss Bain? You look pale. Is it troubling you?'

How did he guess it was throbbing, more now than earlier in the day? But Petra shrugged and answered, 'It's probably because I'm beginning to feel the effects of an almost sleepless night, Mr. Stoddart.'

'But when you did sleep, you slept deeply.'

Jenny looked from one to the other. 'How does Alaric

know? Petra, you didn't—'

'It's not quite what you're thinking, Jen,' said Jay. 'Alaric doesn't work that fast. His technique is to take his time. With his money and his influence he can afford to.' At her puzzled expression he explained, 'I had an accident with the car. Alaric played Sir Galahad and rescued Pet from my wreck on four wheels and drove with her through the night. They slept – and I have his word for it, nothing else – in the back of the car.'

'Together?' Jenny looked at Petra. 'And he didn't make a pass at you, not one single pass?'

'*Jennifer!*' Her brother's voice cracked out. 'Get the hell out of here. All of you, your precious Petra included.'

Like three naughty children they turned and fled.

Darkness brought rain and a coolness to the air. Petra pulled the curtains as the internal telephone rang. It took her a few minutes to find the source of the ring. She found it on the floor behind the settee.

'Jenny here,' the voice said. 'Were you upstairs?'

'No, just looking for the telephone.'

Jenny laughed. 'Sorry, I should have told you. I keep meaning to ask the boss for a table to put it on. Talking of boss, he's asked me to request you to join us for dinner.'

The wording of the invitation might have been Jenny's but Petra doubted it. It irked her, because like so many of Alaric Stoddart's requests it was really an order. She had no wish to keep renewing her acquaintance with the master of the house. The man, with his harsh words and hard, cold manner, should have repelled her, but to her dismay the effect he had on her was the very opposite. So she pleaded tiredness and an aching head.

'Please thank him, Jenny. I appreciate his thought, but I'm just not hungry.'

The phone must have been taken from Jenny's hand because Alaric's voice rapped out, 'I'll get some food sent across to you, Miss Bain.'

'No, thank you, Mr. Stoddart. I'm just not h—'

'I've heard that before. Only a few hours ago, in fact. I

didn't believe it then and I don't believe it now. Despite your protestations, you ate a hearty breakfast.'

'But, Mr. Stoddart, I really don't want—' The man had gone.

The food came on a tray carried by a maid, followed by the short, motherly figure of Mrs. Osborn. 'Mr. Stoddart told me you weren't feeling too good, my dear.'

Petra protested that she shouldn't have bothered, but the housekeeper was opening a gate-legged table and telling the maid to put the tray on it. Then she dismissed the girl.

'You go upstairs, Miss Bain, and get into you night clothes and dressing-gown, then you can sit in front of the fire – I'll make it up before I go – and you can really relax and enjoy your meal.'

Petra was too tired to argue, so she did as she was told. Mrs. Osborn had gone by the time Petra returned. Near the fire, keeping warm, was a pot of coffee, fragrant-smelling and steaming from the spout. On the tray was fruit juice and a salad made by someone with appetite and its appeasement in mind.

After her meal, Petra put aside the tray and curled up on the sinking softness of the settee. In a corner a standard lamp shed a muted yellow light. The fire, piled with logs, splashed sunset red and orange over the cream-painted walls. She pummelled a cushion into place behind her head and sighed, fitting herself into its hollow, letting the luxury, peasant-simple and basic though it was, seep into her tired limbs.

She was warm, replete – a rare experience for her – and relaxed in every muscle. Alaric Stoddart could have his stately home. This simplicity, these artless, supremely natural surroundings were all she wanted. How could she ever want more?

Idly her hand reached out to take up the catalogues and pamphlets about Underlings which Jay had given her to study. There again was the magnificence, the grandeur, that Jay and Jenny had shown her that afternoon, but flat, without the life they had breathed into it.

Petra studied the books for a while, then closed her

71

eyes, only to open them again when people passed by outside. They were laughing and chattering and as their voices died away, she noticed the shadows in the corners of the room. There seemed to be voices again, of people laughing and talking all round her, voices from the past, coachmen, horses neighing, the rattle of wheels on a cobbled yard.

There was a man handing a woman into a carriage. Her fair hair was piled high and she wore a red velvet cloak. He was dark-haired and dark-eyed and as the woman turned to smile at him he did not smile back. Instead, he pulled her head down and placed his mouth on hers, giving her the kiss she seemed to have been asking for, and she was content.

'Petra?' the man even knew her name. How strange, because the woman she had been watching had been herself. But he – who was he? 'Petra?' There it was again. The man was addressing her, so she must respond. She mumbled something and realized she had been talking in her sleep.

When she opened her eyes, she saw him standing beside the settee, looking down at her. His hands were in his pockets and in the flickering firelight she could see he was still not smiling. The man from the past, whom she seemed to know so well, had turned into this cynical-looking stranger, cold-eyed and distant. Alaric the Second she had called him, King Alaric, monarch of all he surveyed. He was surveying her now, but he was not her 'monarch' or her 'lord'. He was her boy-friend's brother, soon, too soon, to be her employer.

'I wouldn't have woken you,' he said, 'but you seemed restless, troubled almost. Is the bruise hurting?' His hand reached out, but she drew her head away.

'It was a dream, nothing else. My head's aching a little, but that's only to be expected.'

'You're stoical about it. How is it you can shrug off pain?'

'My training as an actress, probably, "the show must go on" approach which all actors and actresses learn from their teachers at an early stage. You see,' she smiled up at

72

him, 'drama school has some virtues, you must admit.'

'I admit nothing. You probably developed the ability to endure as a result of your upbringing. Talking of upbringing, is it good manners to turn down an invitation to dine on false pretences?' He looked at the tray. 'You "weren't hungry", you said, but there's not a crumb left. Every time I've given you a meal it's been the same. No wonder you're so pale. It's not, as I thought last night, a result of shock after an accident. It's a permanent look you have about you – of fragility, almost certainly brought about by malnutrition.' He looked her over. In self-defence she pulled her housecoat tighter. 'You're too thin,' was his verdict.

She asked the fireplace, 'For your taste, or for my health?' Then she gave him a quick smile.

He sat on the settee beside her curled-up legs and lowered his head on to a cushion behind him. 'I think you're being provocative. In the circumstances, you're so vulnerable I wouldn't advise it. I might misconstrue it and then you'd be in trouble. No Jay to fight for your honour. Never provoke a male Stoddart. Where women are concerned, through the centuries they've always been quick to respond. One could almost fill a book with the names of past illegitimate Stoddart issue.'

He turned his head and contemplated her, watching her colour rise, turning her pale cheeks to scarlet. 'I'm sorry.' She drew her legs a little nearer, a little farther away from him. The Stoddart magnetism was working again and it tantalized her.

'Don't apologize,' he said lazily. His eyes were occupied with watching the leaping flames, but she felt his mind was elsewhere. 'Only next time, make your meaning clear – for your own sake.' His hand reached out and she held her breath. How right he was to imply that she was at his mercy! But he merely took an Underlings booklet from her lap. 'Reading this to impress me?'

'How could I, when I didn't know you were coming?'

'If you don't bolt your door, it's almost an open invitation. But perhaps you were expecting Jay?' An eyebrow rose.

'I was expecting no one,' she snapped, 'you least of all.'

'Never get angry with your employer,' he said blandly, flicking through the glossy brochure. 'He's the provider of your bread and butter. In retaliation he might leave the "butter" off your bread.' He turned his head and smiled, seeing her struggle to hold on to her temper. 'If you're still suffering from the effects of my brother's careless driving, would you like to delay your start in your new job? A day or two's rest would probably help you recover.' As she shook her head he said, 'It's no picnic working in that tea room. You need stamina. If the other girls see you lagging behind they'll resent it – and rightly. They'll let you know it too.'

'Don't worry,' she said coldly. 'I'll pull my weight. I can work, really work, if I have to. I've learnt the hard way. In any case, I must start to earn my keep, I can't live any longer on your charity.'

'How can you call it charity? Leaving aside the fact that you're going to work for me, you're also my brother's girl-friend. One day, who knows, you might even be part of the family. It's therefore up to me to provide you, gratis, with food and shelter. In any case, I'm not complaining. I'm surprised you have a conscience about it. In my experience most women don't.' He smiled down at the booklet. 'When you start draining me down to my financial reserves by your voracious eating habits, I'll soon let you know.'

She swung her legs to the floor, removed the cushion and drew herself into the corner it had occupied. There were at least twelve more inches between them now. He watched her jerky, nervous movements for a moment, then returned to flicking the pages in his hands.

'I'll be able to eat my fill, won't I,' she muttered, glaring at the flames as though they had done her an injury, 'working in the tea room. I could duck behind the counter in between serving customers and clearing cluttered tables and washing up and I could stuff myself in secret with sandwiches, crisps and cakes.'

'Sorry now you accepted my offer?'

'No. I'm not the sort who jibs at doing an honest day's work, however menial it is. My background precludes that. When there's scarcely enough money in your pocket to live on, you find in yourself an awful lot of humility.'

He threw aside the booklet, folded his arms and stared into the fire for a long time. Then he got up, threw a log on the flames and turned.

'Forgive the question, but,' his thick eyebrows drew together, 'how are you placed for money? Because if necessary I can give you a loan in advance of your weekly wage.'

'Thank you,' her head lifted, her shoulders straightened, 'but I'll manage.'

'Will you?' His manner was brusque. 'You've probably forgotten that you'll have to eat in the staff canteen – yes, I can see you had – and although breakfast is provided free and a special reduction is made in the cost of lunch and the evening meal, you'll still have to pay for them, not to mention tea and coffee breaks during the day.' He put his hand inside his jacket as if feeling for his wallet.

'No, thank you,' Petra repeated. 'If I need a subsidy I'll ask Jay. I've borrowed from him many times before and he from me.'

'And if you ask Jay,' Alaric said, 'he'll borrow from me so that he can give it to you.' He opened his wallet and pulled out a handful of notes, but she shook her head. She refused to accept money from him. 'Come on, girl, don't be so damned proud. This is a loan, not a gift. If you have no money, you won't eat properly.'

'I'm conditioned to that.'

'And,' he went on as if she hadn't spoken, 'if you don't eat properly, you won't work efficiently, and that would hardly be fair to the others.'

He put the money on the table and she looked at it as if he were offering her stolen goods. She thanked him grudgingly.

He nodded and said, 'You know that the day after tomorrow the visiting season opens and that tomorrow the tea room is prepared for use? The local girls who usually staff it will move in. The place is scrubbed from top to bottom, the walls washed and the tables and chairs, too. The manageress, who has already ordered large quantities of food, will be there to receive it when it's delivered.' He paused and their eyes met. 'It's hard work, Petra. The village girls are strong and healthy, well fed and robust in mind and body. I'm not entirely convinced you're the same. You realize what you're taking on?'

She wondered at his odd concern for her welfare and repeated as if taking the oath in a courtroom, 'I realize what I'm taking on.'

'And it doesn't worry you?'

She took a long time to answer. 'Well, it does a little, but,' she looked up at him smiling, 'I doubt if I'll collapse under the strain.'

He did not return her smile. At the door he said, 'Goodnight, Petra,' adding softly, 'I'm sorry I disturbed your dream.'

As the door closed behind him, words floated up from the depths of her mind. When they broke surface and formed themselves into a comprehensible pattern, her heart nearly stopped. 'You were my dream,' they said.

CHAPTER FIVE

As Alaric Stoddart had said, working in the tea room was not easy. Petra washed and scrubbed and polished, had her meal breaks and scrubbed again. At lunch one of the girls called Tess asked her what she was doing there. 'Not one of us, are you?'

Thus, thought Petra, neatly putting me on the other side of the hedge, as if I were a sheep that had strayed from someone else's field.

'You don't look like us,' the girl persisted, 'or talk like us.'

'Sorry about that,' said Petra with a smile, then decided to tell her the truth. 'I'm an out-of-work actress.' Would that touch the girl's heart?

'An *actress*? Did you ask Mr. Stoddart for a job?' Tess looked horrified. 'No wonder you're here, doing hard labour! Ever heard what he thinks of actresses? Everybody in the village knows.'

'I did hear,' said Petra weakly, 'that the Stoddarts have suffered from them in the past.'

'And the present, dear,' said a girl with long black hair called Diane. 'Old man Stoddart's up to his ears in 'em. At his age!' She giggled. 'He'd like you, even if the boss doesn't!'

Everyone seemed to know the Stoddarts' business as well as the Stoddarts themselves. She supposed these girls had been born and bred in the shadow of Underlings, their mothers had probably worked for the Stoddarts and their mothers before them, and so on, back through the centuries. The prospect was daunting. No wonder they looked on her as an outsider, not 'one of them'.

Jay called in and found her washing the walls. He said, 'Good grief, Pet, I didn't bring you here to do this. I should have known my dear brother's tactics. Wear you down until you're begging for mercy, then when he doesn't give you any, fold his arms and watch you walk out. Thus neatly getting rid of you.' He put his arm round her, but Petra twisted away. 'Don't do that, Jay,' she whispered, 'you'll get me a bad name amongst the girls, and their mothers, and their grandmothers, and their great—'

'All right, darling, you've made your point. But it makes me mad to see you doing this sort of work.' She gave him a push towards the door and he murmured in her ear, 'See you this evening. Come to dinner. Jen's going out and I can't stand the thought of sharing the table with my brother and no one else.'

Dinner, with the family? She recoiled at the thought. 'Sorry, Jay. I'm an insignificant employee now, I can't mix with the sons of the owner.'

'Don't be daft,' he hissed. 'Come to dinner.' She shook her head. 'I'll come to you, then.' He went out, having placed a kiss on her ear.

'You sweet on him?' Tess was beside her, giving her an odd look.

'We're – we're friends.' Petra added, feeling an irritated need to justify the relationship, 'You know he's an actor? That's how I met him. We work together—'

Tess nudged her. 'Anything else together?'

Petra smiled, doing her best to look worldly-wise as it seemed the girl wanted her to. Then she shook her head. Obviously Tess did not believe her, because she went on, 'The young one's all right. I wish you luck with him. I could go for him myself. But don't get sweet on the boss, will you? You'd be wasting your time. The fabulous Lady Yvette's got him just where she wants him.' She put her thumbs one on top of the other, indicating that the lower one represented Alaric Stoddart. But Petra found it impossible to believe that the heir to Underlings was under anyone's thumb, and certainly not a woman's.

'Miss Bain and Tess,' called Mrs. Kelly, the manageress, 'there's the floor to be scrubbed, so stop talking and get on with your work.'

So Petra and Tess filled pails, found brushes and scrubbed the floor, Tess taking the inner section and Petra the area near the door. It was late afternoon and she was tired. Her arms were aching from all the work she had done. The brush in her hand seemed to be moving more and more slowly, despite her efforts to make it speed up.

Eventually it came to a stop and Petra sat back on her heels, putting the brush in the pail and moving her hair back from her face. She contemplated the area she had cleaned and compared it critically with the space that remained to be done. The clock high on the wall told her there was another half an hour to go before the working day was officially over. The remaining floor space would take someone like Tess ten minutes to finish, but Petra knew it would take her all of that half hour.

She held her head, but her arms ached too much in that position, so she let them hang by her sides trying to relax every muscle as she had been taught to do at drama school. She sighed and heard a low, warning hiss from across the room. Tess was nodding her head towards the entrance. Petra followed her eyes and came up against a tall, dark, broad-shouldered figure in the doorway, watching her.

The head of the household asked, his voice brittle with censure, 'Tired, Miss Bain? I did warn you.'

Tired, he asked! Couldn't he see it in every line of her body? The 'I told you so' taunt of his smile lashed her energy into a spasm of revival. '*Tired*, Mr. Stoddart?' Her lips set in a straight line and she lifted the dripping scrubbing brush out of the pail, applying it with a vigour that hurt, but nothing would induce her to restrain her hand from its mad rotary movement over the floorboards.

Even when she knew he had gone she did not stop. Not until she had completed the work she had set out to do did she give in to the exhaustion which made her clench her teeth as she unfolded herself from her kneeling position, remove her overall and leave the tea room as Tess had done long before.

Petra walked past the stables where the other girls were having their evening meal. She wouldn't join them, she wasn't hungry. There was a fire, newly-kindled, spluttering up the chimney when she opened the coach house door. A note said, 'Miss Bain: Logs in the shed, food in

79

the larder and the fridge. Ring me if you want more. Mr. Stoddart's orders. Henrietta Osborn.'

Petra sank on to the settee. What was the man up to? First, she thought, he comes to gloat over me in my near-prostrate state, then he tries to make amends by instructing his housekeeper to give me the kiss of life by overwhelming me with her motherly attentions! It was his conscience, Petra told herself, his guilty conscience at her almost collapsed state in the tea room. But – she lay back against the cushions – as an explanation it wasn't entirely convincing. He didn't seem the sort of man to have a conscience, and certainly not a guilty one.

The food, she thought, closing her eyes, she would pay for it. She would not accept charity from the man, so that he could remind her of it any time he had her at a disadvantage – which was, as far as she could see, going to be frequently if the present arrangement continued for long.

The internal telephone shrieked into the flame-loud silence, bringing her across the room at speed.

'Pet? Jay. I'm on my own. Alaric dined alone and left on his ritual rounds of the Underlings guides living in the village. Every year he calls on them personally and discusses rotas and so on. Jenny's out, so I've cancelled dinner and I'm coming over.'

'But, Jay,' her voice wavered, she couldn't help it, 'I'm deadly tired. I can hardly stand on my own feet. I couldn't possibly entertain—'

'Who's asking you to entertain? Me, of all people, who've shared your sandwich and chocolate bar crouching in front of a landlady's gas fire trying desperately to keep warm! All I want is company, your company. I'll scrounge some food from Mrs. Os.'

'Don't do that, Jay. I've got a larder and fridge full of it. Orders of the master of the house, according to the note Mrs. Osborn left me. Come and share whatever it is. I haven't looked yet.'

'You mean she had Alaric's authority? You're kidding!'

'It's true. He saw me almost flat out on the tea room

floor today. Must have thought it would reflect on his image as the perfect employer if one of his staff fainted dead away through overwork!'

When Jay arrived, he found Petra at the cooker frying eggs and bacon. He breathed in deeply. 'Now that's what I call an inviting smell. Let's have breakfast for tea! But *I'm* going to do the cooking.'

He untied the apron from her waist and tied it round himself. He removed the utensils from her hands and led her into the living-room, lowered her on to the settee and lifted her feet on to a stool. 'My brother, the villain of the piece, works you almost to death. I, with my heroic tendencies, rescue you and bring you back to life! Stay there until I come and feed you.'

They sat side by side on the settee, using the coffee table for their plates of food. Jay found an apple tart in the fridge and a jug of cream. They ate it between them. 'I'll invite myself here every evening, Pet, if this is the way you entertain your guests.'

'First,' said Petra, drinking the last of the coffee Jay had made, 'as you said yourself, you aren't a guest, you're a friend. Second, it wasn't my food you ate, it was your brother's.'

'Don't worry, love, he'll probably deduct it from your wages.'

'You could be right. All the same, I'll offer to pay.' Jay told her not to be so stupid, but she said, 'I'm not taking anything from your brother, not a single thing!'

'You really do hate him, don't you?'

Petra shrugged. Did she hate the man? 'I hardly know him well enough to tell whether I've got any feelings for him at all.'

'But you've spent a night with him.'

Petra responded, shocked, 'Not in that way, Jay.'

'Sorry, Pet. I had to be sure.' There was a stiff silence and Jay said, 'It's just that I know my brother. He gets everything he wants. He's had it the easy way all his life. It's the same with women. He's got a certain charm if he cares to exercise it,' Petra remembered the blonde receptionist in the hotel and silently agreed with Jay, 'and if he wants a particular woman, he usually gets her. There may have been exceptions, but only he knows that. We see the ones who don't get away.'

'Yvette?' Petra asked the flames. 'Does he want Yvette?'

'Well, he sees her every time he goes to London, but whether it's just to amuse himself or whether it's the real thing, no one knows.'

Now the flames riveted both their eyes, until Petra yawned, taking herself by surprise. 'Jay, I'm so sorry. I'm not a very good hostess, am I?' She sank back and closed her eyes.

Jay got up and switched off the main light, leaving only the standard lamp on in the corner. Then he threw some logs on to the fire, darkening the room a little more. He removed the receiver from the telephone and bolted the door. He lifted Petra's feet on to the settee, making room for both of them. She protested when she saw his intention, but he soothed her by whispering, 'Go to sleep, sweet.' But she shook her head.

He put his arms around her and kissed her. For a few minutes she submitted, then afraid that he would take advantage of her extreme fatigue, she tried to push him away.

'Let me make love to you, Petra,' he pleaded, but she shook her head violently. 'Marry me, darling.'

'No, no, Jay.' How could she have let the situation get so out of control? 'What would we live on? Where would we live? We haven't got jobs, we've no possessions, at least, I haven't . . .'

'I've got an allowance, Pet.'

'I know, and you spend every penny of it almost as soon as it arrives each month. You've told me.'

'I swear from now on I'll save every penny.'

'How can you when you've nothing else to buy your food with, or pay for the rent of your rooms or your fares to and from auditions?'

'If I knew you were going to be my wife, I'd redouble my efforts to get work.' He pulled away as if he were going there and then, but she held him back.

82

He laughed, as if he had gained a point. 'See, you don't want me to go.'

She protested that he had read too much into what had been purely a reflex action, but he would not believe her. He kissed her again and she pleaded with him to let her sleep for half an hour. 'No longer, Jay. It would take the edge off my tiredness. Then I'll be able to talk sensibly—'

'And say you'll marry me, penniless though I am.'

'It's not that, Jay, it's – it's so many things.'

He shook her a little. 'You love me, don't you, Pet? You love me?'

But she took refuge in silence. Warm in his arms which were loosely round her, she drifted into sleep. It was some time later that she became conscious of having grown restless and was moving her head as if to throw off something that tormented her. She dragged herself from her dream which was sucking her back into it like a perilous bog and awoke to find Jay's lips on hers, kissing her with a petulant passion that frightened her because he had never kissed her that way before. She twisted away and gasped,

'Stop it, Jay. Why – Why—?'

There was a hammering on the door and a hand was doing its best to find a way of opening it. Jay cursed, dragged himself off the settee and unbolted the door which opened straight on to the cobbled yard outside.

'Alaric! What the hell—?'

'I could say the same to you,' was the tart reply. He looked past Jay and saw Petra in the semi-darkness swinging her legs to the floor and pushing madly at her hair to get some order into it. She knew she was dishevelled and knew, too, what Alaric Stoddart was thinking. He came into the room and did not bother to hide his contempt. 'But now,' he said, 'I see the answer to the question I didn't ask.'

'Then you've got the answer wrong,' Jay snapped. 'Ask and I'll give you the correct one. Anyway, what do you want?'

'You. But I wouldn't have come if I'd known I was

interrupting a man and,' with a low bow to Petra, 'a woman in their finest hour.' He raised his right hand. 'Never let it be said that I, Alaric Stoddart, was a spoilsport.' Then he turned his back on Petra. 'You're intending to act as a guide, aren't you? I tried phoning your room. No reply. I tried all over the house with the same result. I tried phoning here but got the engaged signal every time. So I drew my own conclusions,' he looked at the telephone across the room, 'and they were right. Receiver off. No interruptions. Door bolted. Incommunicado. Don't blame you, boy. Take whatever's offered is the old Stoddart motto.' He turned and stared insultingly at Petra. 'If ever I got the green light from that direction, I certainly wouldn't say no.'

But Petra did not rise to his challenge. She sat, head in hands, fair hair hanging forward hiding her face.

Jay said, 'Leave her alone, she's tired out.'

'Having had the pleasure of your company, brother, I'm not surprised.' Jay started to remonstrate, but Alaric cut him off with, 'Never mind, Miss Bain, when we've finished our discussion, he'll be free to return. I may be his big brother, but I don't lock him in his room every night, so he can spend the hours of darkness with any woman he chooses. Come on, Jay,' he turned impatiently to the door, 'Jenny's home. She's waiting for us.'

But Jay went across to Petra, lifted her chin and brushed his lips against hers. 'Want me to come back, sweet?'

She shook her head, aware of Alaric watching in the background. She put her hands up, pulled down Jay's head and kissed him on the forehead. 'Thanks for being so kind,' she whispered. 'And for cooking my tea. Sorry I went to sleep.'

'Are you coming? Alaric rasped from the doorway. Jay lifted Petra's hand, pressed it to his mouth, let it go and followed his brother out.

Work in the tea room began early, when the food for the day was prepared. The public was admitted from ten o'clock onwards for morning coffee and they continued to arrive for meals until the doors closed at six o'clock in the evening.

Jenny put her head round the door. 'Can you spare a minute, Pet?'

Petra noticed how quickly Jenny had fallen into Jay's habit of shortening her name. Outside, Jenny said, 'My two brothers had a hell of a row over you last night.'

Petra's heart misfired. 'What about, Jenny?'

'Jay said Alaric had only put you in the tea room to wear you down and get rid of you. He said you weren't terribly strong – Alaric said that was nonsense because anyone with a grain of common sense could see it was malnutrition you were suffering from and that every time he'd fed you you'd eaten like a ravenous wolf, which proved his point.'

Petra coloured, unable to deny the truth of the statement.

'Then,' Jenny went on, 'Jay said last night you were worn out with overwork. Alaric said judging by the circumstances in which he'd found you both, it wasn't the work that was wearing you out, it was Jay. Jay said that was slander at which Alaric laughed his head off. Then he said that Jay shouldn't have acted as a recruiter of staff by proxy and that having had "the girl" wished on him he had to put her somewhere. Alaric said if only she – you, that is – had had the decency to contact him, Alaric, before planting yourself on the doorstep, as it were, he could have told you straight away there was nothing doing and saved you the journey and the bang on the head.'

'But,' Petra said, recalling the scene in the hotel room, 'I offered to go home. I went to the door, but he called me back. If there wasn't any job, why did he do that?'

'Well, he told Jay he could hardly send an injured girl packing, so he was stuck with you. Anyway, if he had, and since Jay was the cause of your injury, you might have brought a court case against them and demanded damages for injuries received.'

Petra turned crimson and drew in her lips. 'It's no good, Jenney, I'll have to leave. Your big brother doesn't

85

like me. Jay could be right that Alaric only put me here in the tea room to get me off his back. It was only through the kindness of Jay's heart that I came at all. I can't be the cause of a family row.'

'Please don't leave yet, Pet,' Jenny pleaded. 'Jay would hit the ceiling. He's fond of you. He'd accuse Alaric of throwing you out. There'd be an even worse family row.'

'I can't help it, Jenny. In all the circumstances, it's best if I remove myself from Underlings.'

Jenny looked horrified. 'Don't do that!' She looked at her watch. 'Must go now. The hordes are descending any minute. Look, Petra, we must talk about this. In the meantime, don't do anything rash.' She raised her hand. 'See you. Keep smiling!'

When the tea room closed and after the last cups had been stacked away, Petra let herself into the little house she had grown to regard as 'home' and dropped on to the settee. Before confronting the master of the house she must rest, take the weight off her feet, her aching feet, and find sufficient courage to tell him of her decision. What was it he'd said about her? That she was wished on him, that he was stuck with her, that she might claim damages for injuries received . . .

Her legs swung back to the floor and with her feet she felt for her shoes, pushing them on and disregarding her aching muscles. She ran a comb through her hair, but flung it down. Why should she make herself look attractive for that monster of a man?

He stood as she entered his office. He was wearing thick-rimmed spectacles which added to his aloofness. They did nothing to spoil his hard good looks but contributed considerably to his intimidating, autocratic air.

His suit was dark and expensive-looking, his tie, by contrast, dazzled through the intermingling of brilliant colours. He looked at her curiously, said a toneless 'good evening' and added that he had been about to ring her and ask her to come and see him.

She opened her attack at once. 'Wasn't that a little

dangerous, Mr Stoddart?' An eyebrow rose, but the owner of the eyebrow waited for further developments. So Petra expanded her theme. 'Didn't it occur to you that I might claim damages for the injury I received as a result of Jay's accident? Or that I might extort money from you under the threat of phoning the local newspaper and filling the front page with the story of the drunken driving of the younger son of the owner of Underlings, plus a picture of myself revealing my bruises to a gaping, unbelieving public? Thus perhaps securing for myself an acting job as a result of the publicity?'

Alaric's eyes glinted. 'So Jenny's been talking. Or,' the eyes narrowed, 'was it Jay?'

Petra did not reply. He motioned her to sit down, but she remained standing. 'I'm leaving, Mr. Stoddart.'

'So you can't take it, Miss Bain? No, I thought you wouldn't stay the course. I warned you it was hard work.'

'I can take the hard work. It's the insults unlimited I can't – and won't – take. Since you can't rid your mind of your preconceived ideas about me, and since according to you I *wished* myself on you, I'm doing the only decent thing. I'm walking out of the job you manufactured for me. I'm cutting myself loose from around your neck and going back where I came from. Which, knowing your opinion of female members of the acting profession, you would probably say is under the carpet.'

'Will you *sit down*, Miss Bain?'

The suppressed anger in his tone and glance effectively quietened her and she complied.

'Now.' He clicked his pen shut and pushed it into his pocket. He removed the receiver from the telephone. Then he clasped his hands on his blotter and said, 'I see you've come to do business. In your impecunious state, I don't blame you. You want me to make it worth your while to stay. Name the sum.'

Petra shot out of the chair and hit the door with some force. She sought for the handle, but as her hand found it Alaric's hand came down on hers, numbing it by brute force into stillness. 'All right, you've gratified your ego by that show of righteous indignation. Now will you sit down?'

Their eyes met, caught fire, blazed, but the conflagration was short-lasting. Petra looked at his hand bruising hers and as the pain came through her eyes watered, putting out the fire. 'I'll sit down,' she whispered.

He let her go, but before resuming his seat he turned the key and pocketed it.

'All I want,' she said dully, nursing her hand, 'is to be allowed to leave.'

'I'm sorry. That I cannot agree to.'

Her eyes, without a spark of animation, found his. 'I don't know what you mean.'

'No? Well, I'll tell you. I'll tell you that if you go, my brother is so in love with you he'd go with you.' With a violent shake of the head she hoped to persuade him that he was wrong, Jay was not in love with her ... was he? She remembered his words as they lay together on the settee. 'Marry me, darling ... Let me make love to you ... From now on I'll save every penny ...'

How deep did it go with Jay? Against this man, he was as immature as a young boy. Was he playing a part – the great lover, the successful seducer? Emulating his brother Alaric in his alleged and numerous *affaires de coeur?*

'While I could, if necessary, manage without you,' the master of the house continued, 'I couldn't at this time of the year do without my brother's experience as a guide. It therefore goes without saying that even if it costs me a fortune to keep you here, I cannot at present let you go.'

He removed his glasses and laid them aside and Petra caught the full impact of his eyes. 'Tell me something, Miss Bain. Why won't you marry him? Has he asked you?'

Petra answered quietly, 'I resent your intrusion into what is entirely my private affair.'

'Resent away, but I dispute your contention that it's your affair alone. It takes two. My brother is also involved. I repeat, has he asked you?'

'A number of times. But I've never really taken him seriously.'

'My brother must be delighted at your assessment of his integrity.'

'It's not that. It's just that – well, he's a bit too young—'

'Too *young*? At twenty-three?' He put his spectacles into their case with a snap and slipped them into his pocket. 'Why aren't you honest and admit he hasn't enough money, he's too poor for you?' She tried to protest, but he went on, 'You can't deny that every time he talks about marriage you mention his lack of money, his inability to earn sufficient to keep you in comfort, if not luxury. I know this because he told me last night when I tackled him on the subject.'

It was true, Petra had to admit, but this man was twisting her words to mean something sinister, implying she was acquisitive and grasping. 'And *you* must surely acknowledge, Mr. Stoddart,' she said, 'that any marriage haunted by poverty is doomed, however much the parties involved may love each other.'

'Do you love my brother, Miss Bain?'

The question winded her. How could she possibly answer it? Tell him, 'Yes, I love your brother'? But that wouldn't be true. Tell the truth – 'No, I don't love Jay?' In which case he would ask, with good reason, 'then why are you here?' To which she would have to reply, 'To earn some money, no more, no less.' Then he would accuse her of being calculating and callous, of 'using' his brother, of exploiting Jay's fondness for her ... There would be no end to his misguided accusations.

She temporized, 'I'm – I'm fond of Jay.'

'So you still won't commit yourself?' He watched her closely. 'Suppose I tell you in strict confidence that on reaching the age of twenty-five he, and of course Jenny, will receive an allowance considerably in excess of what they get now? And that if Jay were to marry before that age, I would be willing, out of my own pocket, to subsidise both of you so that you could live in the comfort you demand and consider your due. Would that intensify your "fondness" for him and make it change into love?'

She floundered, out of her depth. 'I'll – I'll think about it.'

'You'll *think* about it?' He hammered on the desk. 'You're out for higher stakes? You want me to raise the bid? My God, I didn't bargain for having to deal with such a cool, scheming customer.' He stood. 'All right, I'll make a promise. Once you're Jay's wife, I'll make *you* an allowance, too, an allowance equal to his. *Now* will you commit yourself?'

Choking on a sob, Petra ran to the locked door, pulled at it, turned the handle this way and that, then covered her face with her hands, resting her forehead against the wood. 'Let me go,' she sobbed, 'just let me go. That's all I want. To go, to go . . .'

When she had quietened a little he said, 'I'm sorry, I can't let you go.'

Her sobs became muted to a muffled, hopeless intake of breath. That she had broken down in front of this man, had let him see her at her most vulnerable! It would take her a long time, she knew, to forgive herself. Or him . . .

'Petra? Will you sit down?' His voice was behind her, his arm across her shoulders turned her and walked her back to the chair. He gave her a few moments to recover and when she had found the courage to let him see the ravages the tears had left behind, she said, 'I'm sorry. I must look terrible.'

A hint of a smile softened the line of his lips. 'Don't worry, I don't choose my guides on the basis of their looks, only their ability to do the job intelligently and efficiently.'

It took all of fifteen seconds for the significance of his statement to make an impact. She stared, she did not speak, she scarcely breathed.

'I told you I wanted to see you. We have a vacancy for a guide. After one day back at work, Mr. Winters has decided he's too old to cope. How well acquainted are you with the history of Underlings and its inhabitants, past and present?'

Her unhappiness dispersed like a cloud clearing the face of the sun. 'I know it off by heart.'

'Good. Your wages will go up to the level of the other guides. But I'm warning you, it's hard work, every bit as tiring as the tea room and much more exacting. Questions will be fired at you about the history of many of the exhibits, about my ancestors, about the family fortunes. You'll be required to answer them spontaneously and accurately.'

'And if I don't know the answers?'

'Be honest, say you don't know. But don't say it too often. You must make it your business to know. You understand?'

She nodded. 'When do I start?'

He smiled at her enthusiasm. 'Next Tuesday. Mr. Winters has agreed to stay on the rota until the end of this week. In the meantime, will you continue working in the tea room?'

She agreed and he thanked her. He stood. 'You have six days in which to do your homework.'

As he unlocked the door and opened it, Jay came round the corner from the main corridor. He looked from one to the other. 'What goes, Alaric?' Then, 'Pet, you've been crying. Who did that to you, sweetie? My brother? I'll knock him flying if . . .'

Petra linked her arm in Jay's. 'Guess what, I'm going to be a guide after all!'

'Miss Bain?' She turned to Alaric. 'Have you seen round the gardens and park yet? No? Jay, show her round immediately after dinner. Give her the rundown on the place, the gardens, country of origin of the shrubs and so on. It's not unknown for people to ask searching questions about the surrounding area as they're walking round the house.' He closed the door.

Jay touched her puffy eyes. 'Why, Pet?'

Petra shrugged. 'Your brother can be – well, unpleasant at times.'

Jay swung round and made for his brother's door. 'You want me to—' He raised his fist.

Petra laughed at his 'little brother' act and pulled him

back. 'Forget it. I'm too happy to care now. What time will you come for me? And will we walk?'

'Walk? Hell, no I'm not walking all those miles. Pet,' he linked his hands round her waist, 'come to dinner this evening.' She protested that she couldn't, his brother wouldn't like it, she was an employee . . .

'You're my girl-friend. It's ridiculous that I can't ask you to a meal without having to get Alaric's permission.'

Alaric came out of his office and passed them. 'Alaric, I want Pet to come to dinner. She's my girl—'

Petra said hastily, 'No, Jay, but thanks all the same.' Alaric swept on and turned the corner.

'If he weren't my brother,' Jay said between his teeth, 'I'd—' He stopped. 'Going to have your meal now? Got a few crumbs to spare? I'll join you.'

'But, Jay, it's hardly fair to your brother.'

'Damn my brother.'

'I echo that.' Jenny joined them as they walked towards the rear entrance. 'What's happening, you two?'

'I'm eating with Petra. Run away and play, Jen. Keep Big Brother company.'

'If you're eating with Petra, so am I. I'm not in the mood to dine alone with the boss. Can I, Pet?'

'Three's a crowd,' muttered Jay. 'Nobody asked you.'

'Do come, Jenny,' Petra invited. 'What shall we have? I've got cold meat, salad, treacle tart, cream . . .'

'The lot,' said Jay and Jenny together.

And they did, sitting in front of Petra's roaring fire piled high up the chimney with logs arranged like building bricks. Petra's transistor radio played softly in the background and against it they laughed, talked and ate. The phone rang.

Petra said, 'Yes, Mr. Stoddart? They're here, Mr. Stoddart. Well, they're – they're eating, Mr. Stoddart. Yes, my food, Mr. St—' She hung the receiver upside down as if Alaric's voice was about to fall out of it. 'He's gone. He sounded angry.'

Jay made a dive for the telephone. 'I'll give him angry'!' He dialled and, mimicking a woman's voice said, 'Is that you, Mr. Stoddart? Oh, hallo, Mr. Stoddart. Come and join us, Mr. Stoddart!' And he dropped the receiver on to its cradle.

Twenty minutes later, the noise they were making increased to deafening point. They had filled some wine glasses with sparkling glucose drink – there was no alcohol on the premises and it was the nearest thing they could get to champagne, Jenny said – and were toasting Petra's promotion to the rank of official guide when the front door was pushed open.

Petra, Jay and Jenny sat, glasses raised, stiff as statues, guilty as criminals, waiting for the visitor to speak. His eyes went from one to the other, taking their flushed, excited faces, Jay's arm round Petra's waist, the remains of the food, the transistor on the table. He must have felt the warmth, the gaiety, the companionship radiating from the three of them like heat from a fire.

But their warmth did not reach him as he stood, like a stranger, a cold, aloof stranger in the doorway.

CHAPTER SIX

Jay was the first to break the silence. 'Hi, Alaric! What can we do for you?' Thus putting him on the outside, the interloper, the unwelcome intruder.

'Daylight doesn't last for ever, Jay,' Alaric said. 'It's no use showing anyone round the gardens in the dark. Unless, of course,' cynically, 'you have other activities in mind. But that was hardly the object of the exercise. Petra, get your coat. It may be late April, but there's a chill in the air. I'll take you.'

'Hey now, Alaric, you said—' But Alaric went out.

Petra dashed upstairs and picked up the first garment she could find – a cardigan – and went downstairs putting it on.

'I'll wash up, Pet,' said Jenny. 'Don't keep the boss waiting. He's in a mood.'

'Is he ever in anything else?' Jay asked, staring into the fire. 'I was looking forward to taking you.'

Petra, touched, bent down and rested her cheek on his head. 'Tell you what, Jay, I'll imagine all the time it's you I'm with. And when he holds my hand like you do, and kisses me like you do—'

'He'd better not,' muttered Jay.

'Will you be much longer, Miss Bain?' The cold tones from the doorway vied in chilliness with the draught of air which swept in.

Petra, her face flushed, lifted her cheek from Jay's springy brown hair and looked into the freezing eyes. How much Alaric had heard she did not know, but she cursed herself for being so indiscreet. She looked at Jenny who made a face at her brother's back, then at Jay who continued to stare into the fire, and followed Alaric Stoddart out.

They walked past the stables, hearing the pop music and laughter from the resident staff who were living there. Petra thought, 'That's where he would like me to

94

be. Then I couldn't have his brother and sister to tea.'

'The next time,' Alaric said frigidly, 'you invite Jay and Jenny to a meal, would you mind informing Mrs. Osborn? A lot of food has been wasted unnecessarily.'

'I'm sorry, Mr. Stoddart, but I didn't—' Didn't what? Didn't invite them, they invited themselves? No, she couldn't let them down like that. 'I didn't think . . .'

They turned a corner and Petra saw they had arrived at the back of the house.

'Are we going by car, Mr. Stoddart?'

'By car?' He sounded surprised. 'No, we're walking. How can you see the gardens properly if we drive?'

'It's only that Jay said—'

'I'm not Jay.'

Petra sighed loudly. 'No, Mr. Stoddart.' He looked at her quickly but said nothing. Did the man never unbend? Petra thought. Was there no humanity in him? Did he never let his barriers down even when he was with his lady-love?

They approached a bridge spanning the first of a series of terraced lakes which stretched into the far distance. They looked at the water, mirror-like in the evening stillness, watching the reflections mirrored beneath them with a clarity and detail which was breathtaking in its perfection. Down there, like water colour paintings, were the arches of the bridge they were standing on, the foliage of the leaning trees, the exotic colours of the flowers all around. And down there they could see themselves shimmering side by side in the water.

Petra stared at their reflected selves and in a curious way their eyes met in the water. She tensed, gripping the parapet. The Alaric Stoddart down there was almost as attractive as the real man beside her. Was he smiling? She looked up at him, but she was too late. If he had been, the smile had gone. His reflection, it seemed, was in a happier mood than the man reflected.

After a while Petra said, 'I read in the booklet that Capability Brown designed the gardens and park.'

'He did, let me see, two hundred years ago. His work's unmistakable. Remarkable man. The place was in a bad way when he took over. He altered the park radically and many of my ancestors added to his basic design without spoiling it.' He told her of trees that had come from Australia, Canada, Japan and the Caucasus; others from the Gulf of Mexico and Chile, shrubs from North America and Brazil.

They wandered through the arboretum, and the evening sun glowed orange-red above the branches which were coming into bud. Petra wished she were alone. She would have enjoyed the solitude and the silence of this miniature forest so much more if the disturbing man beside her had not been there. Her imagination would have roamed and scampered through the undergrowth like the squirrel which darted across their path; it would have skimmed the treetops with the birds and buzzed amongst the bushes like the insects all round them.

She could imagine as they walked through the rose gardens and crossed the balustraded bridges and stood near the fountains, her face stroked by their gentle spray, that Underlings was hers, the fairy-tale palace as ruled over by Petra Bain, that its jewellery, its tapestries, its priceless paintings all belonged to her . . .

She jerked herself from the little-girl reverie, shocked to discover how much her unconscious mind with its unexpressed longings had betrayed her, how it had broken through all her cherished principles and beliefs.

As they came out into the open, Petra found they were on a path which led through a mass of rhododendron bushes and which in turn opened out on to a wide walk lined with statues perched on a long stone balustrade. Now and then Alaric stopped to talk to men who were tending the gardens.

Outside a giant conservatory filled with tropical plants and exotic flowers Alaric called to a tall, fair-haired young man who was locking the great glass building for the night.

'Meet Martyn Parker,' Alaric said quietly to Petra. 'The man to whom my sister has quite pointlessly lost her heart. His views are not dissimilar from yours.'

Martyn approached with interest in his eyes, but no

welcome. 'You see,' said Alaric, 'he's already identified you with the "upper classes" he so despises.'

Martyn smiled, but it did not last. 'You want me, Mr. Stoddart?'

'Only to introduce you to a young woman who, in many ways, thinks like you. Her name is Petra Bain. She's a colleague of my brother's. If you and she ever got together, you would no doubt contrive to plot the downfall of the entire Stoddart family, estate and fortune.' A smile softened his words.

Martyn was not amused. He put out his hand, but said nothing.

'Hallo, Martyn,' said Petra, using her smile to try to penetrate his defences. She felt deep sympathy for Jenny who had given her heart to such an uncompromising young man. 'I've heard about you from Jenny, of course.'

He nodded, but was not inclined to take his cue and talk about the girl who apparently loved him unrequited. Instead he talked about his work to his employer who revealed a surprisingly intimate knowledge of the subject in the course of the short but highly technical discussion. As Martyn went on his way, he said a polite but stiff goodnight.

'Oh, dear,' said Petra, 'poor Jenny.'

'And might I add,' said the man at her side, 'poor Jay? Isn't his love unreturned by the girl he seems to want as his wife?'

'I'm sorry,' said Petra, apologetic in spite of herself, 'but one can't turn on love like switching on an electric heater. I'm fond of Jay—'

'But you don't love him.'

'I – I just don't know, Mr. Stoddart. I can't tell yet.' She looked at him with appeal. 'You don't dig up a bulb from the earth to see how well it's growing, do you? So I can't take out my feelings for Jay and examine them, register their growth and put them back.'

'You're a cool customer, aren't you? Your relations with him are such that you're his wife in everything but name—'

'It isn't true!' she cried.

He ignored her protest. 'Yet here you are saying you don't know whether you love him.'

She wanted to tell him the truth, the real state of her friendship with Jay, but knew his mind was closed on the subject, that any explanation would be rejected out of hand.

They were approaching a small white stone building standing on a bank above one of the lakes. The moon, almost full, had risen into a darkening sky and its light was reflected by the white stonework of the building, throwing its own reflection, its columns and the statues sheltering in the portico, back into the tranquil lake.

Trees reached over it, bushes nuzzled against it, it was secluded and private and with this man beside her, and in that moon-laden twilight, a little intimidating.

Alaric invited her to follow him up the steps and she sat beside him in the porch which overlooked the lake. The water, which was ruffled now and then by the splash of birds' wings or the diving beak of a swan, looked dark and mysterious.

'This building,' said Alaric, 'is called the Temple of Achilles, so named by one of my ancestors when it was built two hundred and fifty years ago. You know your mythology? Achilles, son of the sea-goddess Thetis, was dipped by his mother in the River Styx to make him invulnerable. But she was forgetful and held him by the heel, keeping it out of the water, and this part remained vulnerable, eventually leading to his death. My ancestor gave this building that particular name because he maintained that all the Stoddarts had their Achilles heel – a weakness in some part of their character.' There was a short silence, then he said softly, 'You think that appropriate, applicable to me?'

'No, Mr. Stoddart,' Petra replied unequivocally, 'I don't think you possess one weak – or vulnerable – spot in the whole of your nature.'

He laughed. 'So you think my defences are impregnable? You think I'm proof against all human weaknesses, feelings – passions?' He was whispering, his voice seductive, caressing. He had no need to touch her to make her heart beat faster. He had only to speak as intimately and as personally as he was doing to make her want to respond with all the feeling of which she was capable, to lie in his arms as she had done in the car.

She shivered. He said at once, 'You're cold? Have my jacket. I did tell you to bring a coat,' a hand came out and felt her shoulder, 'but you ignored my advice.' She protested that she was all right, that she didn't want his jacket, but it was draped round her shoulders all the same.

'It's not the first time, is it, that you've borrowed my jacket? But last time you maltreated it abominably. Are you tired from our walk? Would you like to use my shoulder as you did before?'

She could hear the taunt beneath the words. 'Yes, I am tired and no, thank you, I can do without support.'

'I'm disappointed. I thought I might persuade you to go to sleep in my arms again.'

Petra found the idea so sweet she jerked to her feet and stood between the columns at the top of the steps. 'I'm rested now, thanks. Shall we go back? It's nearly dark.'

He joined her. 'So soon? Here we are, in a situation as romantic as you could ever wish for, as theatrical a setting as you would find in any play, and all she says is "Shall we go back?" Doesn't the actress in you cry out for the right words, a plot to get your teeth into and a handsome male to play Romeo to your Juliet?'

'The actress in me is unfortunately so out of practice she's almost forgotten how to act. In any case,' she glanced up at him, 'I would have at least to feel the beginnings of liking for the man I was acting with.'

He gazed at her narrowly. 'Tell me if I'm wrong, but I imagine that your dislike of me borders on hatred?'

She answered with a smile, 'No employee in her right mind would tell her boss she hates him, would she?'

He laughed and took her arm, propelling her back to the seat. 'Stay a little longer. Tell me, now you've seen the glories of Underlings, both inside and out, its valuables, its parkland, its immense worth, hasn't that helped you to commit yourself where Jay's concerned? Be honest, wouldn't you give your all to become a member of the Stoddart family and share their wordly goods? Hasn't the sight of it evoked in you the faintest spark of envy, of covetousness, of the longing which visitors tell us they experience that the place belonged to them, to people like Petra Bain, instead of Alaric, Jay and Jenny Stoddart, not to mention their father, Sir Titus?'

She bit her lip, remembering the betrayal of her thoughts as they had wandered round the park. She said too quickly, too emphatically, 'Of *course* not! You know my views—'

He laughed, and there was a ring of triumph in the sound. 'You're not telling me the truth. You *have* felt the longing, the wish that it was yours to possess. So the equality-mad, fanatically democratic Miss Petra Bain has her weakness, her Achilles heel!' He went on thoughtfully, 'Of course, if you reject Jay as a possible husband, there is an alternative. Jay has a brother – myself. Underlings could be yours one day, Petra, if you played your cards right.' She hated the taunt in his voice. 'But, unfortunately for you, you would have to accept me as an essential part of the deal. You see, there would be no nonsense of a marriage in name. I should be a demanding, possessive husband . . .'

In the darkness his arm found its way underneath his jacket which swung from her shoulders. His fingers fastened on to her waist, but she jerked away and stood at the top of the steps looking out over the black rippling pool.

'Are you beginning to exercise the ancient Stoddart right of seducing the servants and employees?' she asked bitterly, fighting the feelings of his touch and his words had aroused. 'And aren't you taking a terrible risk in making such a suggestion – that I transfer my feelings from Jay to you? I might find a way round my scruples and my – my dislike of you and take your proposal – surely that's what it was, wasn't it? – as being sincere.' She swung round to face him. 'After all, all women want in life is marriage and money, isn't it? You said yourself.

Poor as I am, even I might consider it expedient to marry a man who means – nothing to me, but who could provide all the comforts any woman could possibly want.'

She ran down the steps, tearing his jacket from her shoulders, as if by doing so she could tear him out of her mind and the tug of him from her body.

He joined her, taking his jacket. Her words had turned him into an enemy again, and they walked back in silence. She thanked him for showing her the grounds and he said stiffly,

'There's a great deal more to see, rose gardens, covered walks, farms and so on. Jay can show you the rest.'

He left her at the door of the coach house and walked away as though he had already put her out of his mind.

The morning Petra began her duties as an Underlings guide, she had an attack of first night nerves. Twenty or so people gathered expectantly in the great entrance hall, holding their guide books and their postcards, cameras hanging from their necks, Underlings engraved pens and pencils in their pockets and handbags.

Petra stood, her dress simple, her shoes flat-heeled and comfortable, hands clasped demurely in front of her, desperately trying to recall what Jay had told her.

'Never lead the way out of one room and into another. Always stand back and let the people pass in front of you so that you can keep a discreet but close check on the activities of individuals who might linger, most with genuine interest but one or two possibly with evil intent.' As she talked to them, Jay had said, her mind mustn't go to sleep. She must act as her own detective, watching, watching all the time.

The crowd grew quiet like an audience waiting for the curtains to part, and she began to recite, monotonously at first, but as she grew less nervous, with light and shade in her voice, the history of Underlings.

She took them along a corridor with an intricate mosaic floor, explaining the origin of some of the paintings which hung on the walls. She told them the story of the name of the great house; about the doubtful activities of

Alaric the First, pointing out the portrait of his father, Sir Cecil, who disowned his son in his will.

In the State Dining Room hung portraits of the present Stoddart family. In the centre was Sir Titus Stoddart, owner and father of the present occupants of the house. Next to him was his late wife, Sylvia. To his father's right was a portrait of the heir to Underlings, Alaric Stoddart, with his twin brother and sister on their mother's left.

The crowd moved slowly along the Dress Corridor, with its collection of ceremonial dresses and outfits worn by the Stoddarts of the past. One dress in particular – the white satin wedding dress – caught the visitors' attention.

'Who's wearing it next?' one of them asked, looking lovingly at the intricate embroidery and lace.

Petra laughed a little uncomfortably. 'Whoever becomes the bride of Mr. Alaric Stoddart, the present heir, I suppose. He's not even—' her eye was caught by a familiar face at the back of the crowd, dark-haired, heavy-browed and listening intently, 'he's not even engaged yet,' she faltered. 'At least, if he is, it's kept a close secret.'

'Is he like his naughty namesake?' an elderly lady asked, quite unaware that the man of whom she was speaking was standing only a few yards from her. 'You know, likes the ladies!'

Petra dared not look at the heir to the family fortunes. 'There – there are rumours,' she said, 'but as far as I know, little evidence to support them.'

As the crowd passed by, Petra kept her eyes on them as she had been instructed to do.

'Very diplomatic,' said a sardonic voice beside her. 'But I would prefer it if you did not discuss my private affairs or those of my family with the visitors, however loaded and persistent their questions might be.'

'I'm sorry, Mr. Stoddart.'

He indicated the fast disappearing group of people and motioned her to follow them, thus subtly reminding her that she had no right to allow them to wander about unattended. She walked in front of him, her head high, her heart pounding with anger that he had seen fit to reprimand her on duty, or to be there listening to her at all.

'All the same,' he said, walking by her side, 'you're doing quite well. Just put a little more life into your descriptions and say the words more naturally and not as though you're a ham actor being put through his paces by the producer of a second-rate play, and by the end of the season, if you last that long, you'll be nearly as good as all the other guides.'

With which sarcastic piece of advice he left her.

The week passed and Petra found herself looking forward immoderately to her day off. Although her hours of work were spread out so that she, in common with the other guides, had reasonable rest periods, she found the act of almost non-stop walking nearly as exhausting as working in the tea room.

Every evening Jay and Jenny invited themselves to share her meal. Alaric, they said, was annoyed. 'But I told him we're big children now,' Jay said, 'and we can eat where we like.'

'Alaric grew mad,' Jenny took him up, 'and said you had no right to expect us to go on keeping you company indefinitely at your evening meal, and even if you did it was up to us to tell you we couldn't.'

'So I told him we preferred to eat with you and if he tried it, he'd like it, too.'

'He said,' Jay continued the tale, 'he never went (a) where he wasn't invited and (b) where he wasn't wanted.'

'Then he said,' Jenny added, 'that if we liked "the girl's" company that much he'd have to tolerate you at dinner now and then just to keep us and Mrs. Os happy. Apparently the cook's getting fed up with having only Alaric to cook for.'

'So,' said Jay, 'there's an open invitation for you to come across and dine with us whenever you feel like it.'

'And if our brother objects,' Jenny said, 'we can always hold over him the threat of eating with you!'

Petra smiled. She couldn't see Alaric Stoddart giving in to any 'threat' from his brother and sister – or anyone else. But she shook her head. 'You'll have to stop coming here and eat with him again. But don't expect me to join you, Jay. I like Jenny's cosy little house too much to want to forsake it and dine in state with the lord of the manor.'

When her free day arrived, Petra got up late, then, for want of something better to do, made a few cakes. Jay and Jenny were on duty all day, so she saw nothing of them.

She was thinking of having some tea when the telephone rang. 'Alaric Stoddart here. I'm tired of my own company every evening at dinner, so in order to keep my brother and sister at home, I'm inviting you to dine with us. Will you please join us?'

Could the man never be pleasant, even when he was issuing an invitation? Perhaps he had phrased it that way to make her refuse. Well, he had succeeded. 'No, thank you, Mr. Stoddart. Like you, I never go where I'm not wanted.'

There was a short, sharp sound from the other end. 'If you can suggest any other way of keeping my brother and sister from accepting your standing invitation to them to eat with you, then I'll willingly take it.'

'I don't invite them,' she was about to say, but found that once again she couldn't let Jay and Jenny down.

'However,' Alaric was saying, 'although I've racked my brains, no alternative has come to me, so I repeat, will you dine with us? Would it make you change your mind,' he paused, 'if I said,' his voice softened and to Petra it was the tone-change of an experienced actor, 'your company was not unwelcome?'

Nevertheless her cheeks grew warm and her heartbeats increased in pace. 'Are you – are you sure, Mr. Stoddart? After all, I'm only an employee, one of your under-lings . . .'

'You're my brother's girl-friend,' he snapped. 'Well, is it yes or no?'

'Yes, thank you, Mr. Stoddart,'

He cut himself off.

But in the family dining-room, Alaric's manners could not be faulted.

Petra found herself relaxing and in spite of herself, responding to the charm she had seen him use on others, but never dreamed would ever be directed at her. Was this his way, she wondered, of making her feel at ease and accepting his invitation again in order to keep his wayward brother and sister from straying from the fold?

Alaric took his coffee alone in his office.

'Does he work every evening?' Petra asked. 'Doesn't he ever relax?'

'Not often,' Jenny said. 'When he does, he listens to music, classical, of course. He says the stuff Jay and I listen to drives him mad.'

'Anyway,' said Jay, pushing back his chair, 'he'll be going away once the visiting season is properly launched. He's never out of London for long.'

'For London,' said Jenny, 'read Yvette. Her tentacles even reach as far as Derbyshire. She calls, he goes.'

'I thought,' said Petra, her heart behaving queerly, 'he has business in London?'

Jay nodded. 'But every businessman needs somewhere to relax. So where better than in Yvette the Beautiful's arms?'

Petra went to the door. For some reason she had to get away – away from that portrait of Underlings' heir, looking down on her so mockingly, so magnetically, so disturbingly.

'What's the matter, Pet?' Jay asked, immediately solicitous. 'Feeling tired? You look pale.'

'Let's cheer her up,' said Jenny, 'counteract the effect dining with the lord of the manor's had on her. Let's have a mini-party.' She looked at her watch. 'Martyn'll be finished work by now. I'll ring him.'

'He won't come,' Jay jeered.

'He will!' Jenny retorted. 'I'll – I'll tell him I want him to meet your girl-friend.'

Petra hadn't the heart to tell her that she and Martyn had already met and he had remained singularly unimpressed.

'Where shall I say, Petra? Your place?'

'It's your place really, Jenny. But what about eats and drinks? Will coffee and cakes do?'

Jay groaned, but Jenny said, 'What better?' To Jay, 'Martyn doesn't drink and I'm not over-fond of the stuff. Petra? No, she's not, either. So you can do without for once. Anyway, you can't take your drink like Alaric can, even though he doesn't often indulge.'

'Big deal for brother Alaric! What harm does it do to have a drop too much now and then?' He slapped his head, remembering the accident. 'Sorry, Pet.' He kissed her, his lips lingering.

The door opened. Alaric, eyes narrow, watched for a moment, then, as they broke apart, gave an ironic bow and started to withdraw, but Jenny called, 'We're having a party. In Petra's place. Coming, Alaric?'

'I'm going to play some records and I was intending to invite Petra to join us in the drawing-room, but no doubt she shares your abominable taste in music. Anyway, I'm the last person she'll want to listen to anything with.' To Petra, with a sudden change in tone, 'Forget I even mentioned it.' He went out.

Jay commented, 'Exit Alaric the Ruler, thwarted for once.'

To Jay's surprise and Jenny's delight, Martyn accepted the invitation. As soon as he arrived, Jenny pounced on him, dragging him to the settee and hanging on to his arm as they sat together. Jay threw himself into an arm-chair and pulled Petra down on to his knee, but she struggled free.

'No, no, Jay, I'm the hostess. You can't monopolize me.'

Jay sulked and Petra went into the kitchen to make coffee. When she carried in the tray of cups and cakes, Jenny appeared to have succeeded in winding Martyn's arm round her waist.

Petra distributed the food and sat in the armchair opposite Jay. Now and then he made frantic 'come over here on my knee' signs to Petra, but she determinedly refused to comply.

Jenny had now managed to wriggle herself into

Martyn's arms and he did not seem to object too strongly. But, watching them, Petra felt that as soon as Martyn was up and away, he would resolutely put Jenny out of his thoughts, even though it might cost him some effort because she was a warm, lovable girl.

Into the laughter, the beat of the music from the transistor, the chatter and the roaring of the log-lapping flames, came Alaric. There was instant silence and both Petra and Martyn, employees now instead of hostess and guest, stood deferentially.

Jenny, her arms empty of the man she loved, snapped, 'What do *you* want, Alaric?'

'An hour or so ago,' he drawled, 'I was invited to a party. At the time I declined. Now I've changed my mind. If the lady of the house,' with a mocking bow to Petra, 'will accept a latecomer, I should like to join you.'

Petra, remembering her role, said, 'Do come in Mr. Stoddart. We'd love to have you. So glad you could come after all.'

'Spoken,' he said sarcastically and making his way across the room to her side, 'like an old hand, like a born hostess steeped in the social graces. You weren't by any chance,' an eyebrow flicked up, 'speaking lines from a play you've acted in?'

Petra, with iron control, held her irritation down like the lid of a boiling kettle. Summoning all her dramatic training to her aid, she said as graciously as a member of the nobility, 'Do sit down, Mr. Stoddart. Please take my chair.'

'I wouldn't dream of it, Miss Bain,' he said, a gleam in his eye. 'If I'm in your play, I insist on acting the part of a gentleman. If this is your chair, I shall share it with you. You sit on the seat, I'll make use of the arm.'

And he did, sliding his arm across the back of it and smiling smugly into Jenny's, and particularly Jay's wide open eyes. He was all brother now, taunting and irritating, absolutely their equal, dropping for the moment his role of boss and father figure.

Martyn subsided on to the couch again, but taking care to put the length of a sprung cushion between himself and Jenny. Petulantly, she closed the gap and slipped her arm into his, but he held it stiffly and she was left holding a rigid limb. She glowered at her elder brother, but he was looking down at Petra, who suddenly remembered her role.

'Coffee, Mr. Stoddart?' She poured him a cup. As she gave it to him, he smiled at her as if not to be outdone by his younger brother. 'Biscuit?' she whispered, responding against her will to the pleasantness in his face, the curve of his lips, the secret meaning in his eyes.

The charm, she thought, he turns on for others, but never, until this evening, on me. Why me now? To make Jay jealous? What game was this maddening man playing?

Petra sat in the chair beside him again. There was no alternative except the floor. Alaric stirred his coffee, scooping out on the spoon a few grains of undissolved sugar and contemplating them as if they were thoughts dredged up from his own head.

He looked at his sister who was clinging to the young man beside her as if at any moment he might take to his heels and disappear out of the room and her life. He dwelt reflectively on Martyn and said,

'I suppose you and Petra here have been busy chewing over the rights and wrongs – mostly the wrongs – of the private ownership of one of Britain's most famous historic houses? I suppose you,' looking down at Petra, 'have as good as given it to a charitable institution, turned it into a hospital or even an educational establishment, and you,' to Martyn, 'have bulldozed it into little bits, having first removed the valuables and handed them over to the nearest museum?'

It seemed he was in a mood to provoke an argument, and Martyn rose to the bait. 'A place like Underlings,' he said, 'is nothing but an anachronism. It's outlived its natural – or unnatural – life. Its only use is to give people with a morbid curiosity something to do when it rains while they're on holiday.'

'Morbid curiosity?' Alaric's eyebrows rose with the question.

'Yes,' Martyn answered shortly. 'The people who go round these places are like birds of prey, coveting the place yet having to comfort themselves with the crumbs they glean from the short, expensive glimpse they're allowed to have of the place. Their egos swell almost visibly as they enter the house because for half an hour or so they imagine themselves into the role of owner, with a family tree like yours going back to the seventeenth century and beyond and an ancestry peppered with lords and ladies, all of whom were probably scoundrels of the first order, but because they were titled and members of the aristocracy they could be forgiven anything, even fraud, forgery and the seduction of all the village maidens who crossed their paths.'

Petra, hearing the bitterness in Martyn's voice, grew afraid, but Alaric laughed out loud. 'Well said, Martyn! An excellent summing-up of the roguery of the Stoddarts through the ages. So you think it's wrong of us as a family to allow such a building to go on standing, and that maintaining it and preserving it is merely throwing good money after bad, that it's no more than a sentimental relic of a golden age that will never come again?'

Martyn nodded vigorously and Jenny snuggled even closer as if to placate him.

'Hasn't it occurred to you that these stately homes, these architectural masterpieces – because that's what they are – are amongst the greatest contribution this country has made to the arts? Yet you dismiss them as merely products of their age, and appreciated only by those in whose day they were created? You're wrong, you know, so wrong. Ask Petra here.' He looked at her and she gazed up at him, her eyes caught by the odd light in his.

Did he love his home so much it moved him to a muted passion, he who appeared to possess no deep feelings, no strong emotions that he couldn't control?

'Against her will,' Alaric went on, 'she's responded to the beauty of the place. Be honest, Petra, and admit it.'

'Yes, I do admit it,' she answered slowly, 'but I still

can't reconcile myself to the fact that it's owned by one family . . .'

'And you think that I – or rather my father – should therefore give it away?' She nodded, still gazing up at him. 'Shall I tell you something? Not all the great houses offered to the Trust are accepted. If the building isn't in danger through decay and neglect, if it can be maintained in good condition by the present owners, then the Trust may well say "No, thanks". So you see, they wouldn't thank the Stoddart family if Underlings was offered to them. We can keep it going at our own expense and we intend to do so as long as we're able.' He smiled. 'Sorry, Petra.' His hand rested on her shoulder. 'Lecture over, but it had to be said.' He looked at his watch and stood up. 'Don't let me break up the party, but I must go.'

Petra, watched by the others, saw him to the door. He put out his hand and she put hers into it. He looked at their clasped hands, started to speak, changed his mind and said, 'Thanks, Petra,' and went out.

Jenny and Martyn left soon after that, but Jay sat on, chin in hand, staring into the dying fire. 'Did you,' he asked, 'have to gaze at him as though you worshipped the ground he walked on?'

Petra sat up stiffly. 'What are you talking about?'

'You. And Alaric. You couldn't take your eyes off him, could you? Every word he spoke you listened to as though they were pearls of wisdom and he was a damned oracle.'

'I didn't,' she said, 'I didn't!'

'You couldn't see yourself. Anyone would think,' he said sullenly, 'you were in love with the man. Oh, I couldn't blame you if you were. He could charm a statue into moving if he tried. All the women fall for him, and he knows it. There's something about him – my God, if I had it—' He got up and pulled her into his arms and kissed her. 'If I had it, you'd be gazing at me like that. You'd have married me long ago, wouldn't you?'

She turned crimson. Was she as transparent as he was making out, were her secret feelings so obvious they were written on her face? And had Alaric guessed? Was that why his manner was so strange as he said goodbye — because he was *sorry* for her for liking him so much? What, oh, what had she given away to him?

CHAPTER SEVEN

PETRA was rarely alone in the evenings. Jenny or Jay, or sometimes both of them, joined her. Sometimes Martyn came, too – he was more at his ease nowadays and Petra felt Jenny might be making some progress with him at last.

The day after the mini-party, Alaric went to London. To Yvette, the twins said, as well as to work. Petra drooped in his absence. She wished she could count the days to his return, cross them off on a calendar or in the pages of her diary. But no one could tell her when he would come home again.

One day Jay asked Petra if she would pose for a photograph wearing one of the dresses displayed in the Dress Corridor. 'We've got a postcard of it displayed on the stand, but Jenny and I think it would be a better buy for visitors if it were modelled.'

'But surely Alaric should be consulted, Jay?'

'Oh,' he said, 'we've talked about it a number of times, but we couldn't find anyone suitable to wear it – no one pretty enough or shapely enough – till you appeared on the scene!'

'But I've never had training as a photographic model.'

'You've learnt how to walk and pose and so on at drama school as well as I have. Lots of actresses do modelling in their spare time. Come on, darling. You'll have all the visitors drooling over the result and who knows, you might even land yourself an acting job by showing it to an agent. There's a professional photographer living in the village longing to get the assignment.'

So, a little fearfully – would she get into trouble with Alaric? Petra agreed to the proposal. Jenny and Mrs. Osborn helped her to put on the dress. It was over eighty years old, delicate and entirely hand-made, and it fitted her perfectly. It was pearl-pink in colour and the hem, the dipped waistline and the sweepingly low neck were covered in minute pearls sewn on to bands of satin. The long sleeves ended in layers of lace and this was repeated at the edge of the skirt which swept the floor.

Jenny found some family heirloom earrings with a pearly necklace to match, combed Petra's hair so that it was clear of her face and fixed a pearl-studded band across the top of her head. Then, with make-up, she brought Petra's face to life.

The photographer stayed most of the morning, taking countless photographs. Petra was told to sit, stand, walk, to turn and look back over her shoulder. It was tiring, but she found it also oddly invigorating. By the end of the photographic session, she felt as if she had taken on the character of the Stoddart ancestor to whom the dress had once belonged.

But the part she had played was over now. She was no longer a well-to-do Stoddart of the past but an impoverished young actress of the present called Petra Bain.

Ten days passed and Alaric still had not come back. Petra would not allow herself to admit how much she missed the sight and sound of him. Then one evening – it was a Friday – she was making her way to the coach house when she saw his car standing in the drive outside the main entrance.

Her heart raced and no matter how much she told herself she was a fool, she could not reason herself out of her excitement. She probably wouldn't see him for days, but he had come home and for her it was enough.

She had her evening meal alone, Jenny and Jay thinking it expedient to dine with Alaric on his first evening back. Petra had not spoken to the twins that day, although they had waved from a distance.

She felt weary. The conducted tours on which she took the eager sightseers made her return to the coach house every evening drained of energy.

She peeled off her dress and slipped into her housecoat. Then she took one of Jenny's paperbacks from the bookshelves, removed her slippers and curled up on the settee.

But the combination of fatigue and the soporific effect of the fire soon had her head against the cushions and her eyes closed.

Somewhere in her dream a door was flung open, and into her quiet sleeping world came a violently angry man. It was not the noise that woke her so much as the charged silence that followed the noise. Her eyes opened and she gasped. His face was white with rage and his eyes blazed down into hers. Dazed as she was from her sudden waking, the height and breadth of him became enormous and menacing.

'I should have known,' Alaric rasped, 'that in refusing my brother's offer of marriage, in declining to commit yourself and admitting to loving him, you'd set your sights on something – someone – higher up the scale. You,' his lip curled, 'with your worship of democracy, your prattle about equality and the unfairness of private ownership of historic houses!'

The attack, unjustified as it was, made the room revolve. If she held herself stiffly, she told herself, searching for the stability of the floor and confronting him, it might stop her from shaking. With her bare feet and the flimsy state of her clothing under her housecoat, she was at such a disadvantage that her poise crumbled and her voice quivered as she asked,

'Will you please tell me what you're talking about?'

'Stop play-acting,' he bit out. 'In doing what you've done, you must have expected – and accepted – all that's coming to you. Did you think I'd open my arms wide for you to walk into them – *uninvited*?'

'Please,' she whispered, shaking her head, 'I don't know what you mean.'

'And you told me you considered yourself a bad actress? That you never got leading parts? If a theatrical producer could see you act as you're acting now, your name would be in lights. Well, by subtle trickery, you've got yourself a leading part. You've wished yourself on me as my fiancée and you're going to take the consequences, every damned thing that goes with the position. Don't you think,' he moved nearer and she could not move backwards because the couch was behind her, 'that since, according to you, we're going to be man and wife, I'd better get to know my future bride a little better? In the hotel you held me off – probably, in the light of what has now happened, to whet my appetite. And,' his eyes moved insultingly over her, dwelling on her inadequate state of dress under the housecoat which had fallen open, 'Stoddart that I am and therefore quick to respond to any display of feminine willingness, my appetite is crying out to be appeased, and you shall be the one to appease it. This,' he gripped her arms, 'is merely a foretaste of what is coming to you now you're my fiancée.'

He twisted her round so that she was lying in his arms, his lips came brutally on hers and the pressure of his mouth forced back her head. She clung to him because if she hadn't, she would have fallen. And still he did not stop. She wanted to free her mouth, she wanted to plead for mercy, but it seemed that her struggles only increased his anger and his cold, ruthless ardour. When he finally relented, he thrust her away as if he had no more use for her and she sank back on to the couch.

She covered her face and her cheeks, which had been burning, now felt cold and ashen. She thought she was going to faint and held her head low. He made no move to help her. Instead, after a heavy, breathing silence, he went on, 'You claim ignorance of the facts, but you can protest as much as you like, I won't believe you. You're cool, scheming and calculating, and I can produce evidence to support this.' He walked up and down the room. 'I've been away a fortnight. This evening I return, dine with my brother and sister, go into my office and there, on my desk, I find today's paper, the local paper. What do I see staring at me from the front page? You. "Miss Petra Bain", the caption said, "beautiful and talented actress fiancée of Mr. Alaric Stoddart, son of Sir Titus Stoddart, Bart., and heir to the world-famous historic house, Underlings." '

He pulled the folded front page of the newspaper from his pocket and held it out. Petra saw a photograph of herself, hands demurely clasped, smiling disarmingly and wearing the pearl-studded Stoddart dress. The report beneath the picture said, 'Here, Miss Bain is modelling a gown worn by one of her fiancée's ancestors. The engagement was a complete surprise to the villagers, to the staff of the Great House as it used to be called and also to the friends and acquaintances of Mr. Stoddart. He and his attractive wife-to-be have made their liaison the secret of the year. Will it also be the wedding of the year?'

'Now tell me you know nothing about it, that the reporter and photographer dreamed up the story – and the picture. Now tell me you were innocent, that you didn't give them all this information, all these lies, that it wasn't your doing.'

What can I say? she thought feverishly. Tell him his brother and sister must be behind it all, must have played a trick on him, probably to annoy him? Why else should they have done it? Without evidence of their complicity, or even with it, she couldn't let Jay and Jenny down when they had been so good to her.

She shook her head helplessly and handed him back the paper, but he crumpled it and flung it across the room. 'Get your things together. You can't stay here. You'll have to have the main guest room and live in the house in surroundings which will suit your elevated status as my future wife.'

Petra looked up at him, aghast at what he was saying. 'But I'm not your future wife. You'll have to issue an official denial.'

He took her by the shoulders. 'Don't try my patience too far. You announce our "engagement", then you expect me to make myself – and you – the laughing stock of the village, the country and the world, by denying it? What should I say, do you think? "Miss Petra Bain, without so much as consulting me, her employer, in my absence made herself into my fiancée. But she's not really my fiancée, she's my brother's close – very close – friend. But because she felt I was a better catch both financially and status-wise, she decided to marry me, to take my name and my fortune, while continuing her illicit relationship with my brother." Is that what you think I should tell the press?'

She said slowly – slowly because it hurt, 'You could announce your engagement – to Lady Yvette. That should kill the speculation stone dead, and save your face. If it makes me look a fool, or even a cast-off girl-friend, I don't mind. I can take it. Your name would be cleared.' Her voice hardened to cover her distress. 'After all, think of the publicity it would bring and all the acting parts I'd be offered as an ex-woman friend – and all that implies – of the heir to Underlings.'

He considered her. 'I've a good mind to take your advice. Yes, I will announce my engagement. I'll ask the lady concerned. Thanks for the suggestion.'

There was a long silence and Petra was glad the fire had burned low and the standard lamp shone, isolated, in a far corner. Alaric would not be able to see the misery of her expression, the dullness in her eyes.

He looked at his watch. 'I have a number of phone calls to make. Where national daily newspapers are concerned, the night is young. I might even catch the first editions. Because Underlings is so well known and because of my position in relation to it, not to mention my connections with the business world, the sooner the announcement of my engagement is made official, the better.'

He went to the door. Petra whispered, 'Goodbye, Mr. Stoddart.' He looked back at her for one agonizing moment and left her.

Petra breakfasted early next morning. She had slept badly and was happier walking about than tossing and turning. There was a discreet tap at the door as she was clearing the table and she went to answer it, teapot in hand.

Mrs. Osborn stood there, her face alight with smiles. 'Miss Bain, my dear, I'm delighted with the news. Congratulations on your engagement. It's in all the papers. Everyone's so pleased. The staff have said all along what a pleasant young lady you are. And you were so quiet about it, pretending you were Mr. Jay's young lady to hide it, I expect! Mr. Stoddart's sent for you, Miss Bain.

Here, give that to me.' She took the teapot from Petra's tightly clenched fingers. 'You mustn't do the household chores now, dear. You're Mr. Alaric's fiancée, can't have you dirtying your hands doing that sort of thing. Later, he says, we're to move all your belongings to the house.'

Petra shook her head. Mrs. Osborn took it as a sign of bewildered happiness. 'You should see how pretty you look in the papers, Miss Bain. It'll be in all the society magazines, not only here, but all over the world. You're famous now, Miss Petra. You'll be so much in demand.'

The phone rang. Mechanically Petra answered. 'Petra?' It was Alaric, and his was not the voice of a man deeply in love. 'I sent for you. Why the delay?'

Petra swallowed. How on earth should she speak to the man to whom the whole world now considered her engaged? Tell him exactly what she thought of him for breaking his promise? Call him "darling" and say, 'I won't keep you waiting another minute, because I love you so much'?

'I'm sorry, Mr. – er – Mrs. Osborn's here. She's been – she's just congratulated me. I – I'll come at once. Sorry to – keep you waiting,' she felt Mrs. Osborn at her elbow, 'd-darling.' The word nearly choked her. She cut off the mocking laughter.

A gentle hand patted her shoulder. 'You're so confused, aren't you, Miss Petra? Not used to it like Mr. Alaric is. I'll take you across to him.'

'No, no, thank you, Mrs. Osborn. I won't trouble you—'

'It's no *trouble*, dear. Anyway, Mr. Alaric's in his private apartment. You probably know where that is now,' she gave a wink, 'but I mustn't let you get delayed by people wanting to talk to you when he's so impatient to see you!'

They seemed to meet the entire staff of Underlings. Maids, lady cleaners, servants of all levels and descriptions, even Alaric's chauffeur, seemed to know and went out of their way to say how pleased they were. It seemed the only person who wasn't was herself.

Mrs. Osborn knocked on a door, listened for a moment

and opened it, indicating to Petra that she should go in. With the housekeeper standing in the background, the meeting had to be convincing, of lovers coming together at last after a long night of separation.

Alaric smiled and held out his arms. He's making me go to him, Petra thought furiously. Bringing all her acting technique into play, she crossed the room, her head high, a falsely brilliant smile on her pale face, and felt his arms wrap about her.

'Petra, my sweet,' he murmured just before his lips closed on hers.

She submitted, she had to, because they had an audience. She fought against the desire to struggle, she fought against the desire to submit utterly and finally to the feelings that set her heart racing at the touch of him.

When the door clicked shut at last, telling them they were alone, she tore herself from him. 'How could you,' she blazed, 'how could you break your promise?'

'I made no promise,' he replied blandly. 'I said I would announce my engagement. I said I would ask "the lady concerned". I didn't specify when, I didn't specify whom. Nor did I mention in which order I would do these things.'

'So it was a trick!'

'No more a trick than the one you played on me, my dear. I said you would take the consequences – every single one – of your action. And I meant it.' He walked towards her. 'Now I shall ask "the lady concerned".' He took her loosely by the wrists, but she tried to escape, so he tightened his grip. 'It's already a *fait accompli,* but will you become engaged to me?'

'No, I will not!'

'Your refusal is a little belated, not to say too late. It won't be for long. Regard it, if you like, as a part-time job. You're an actress by training, so you should carry it off well. Make it the acting chance of your life. I'll even increase your salary. Leading ladies always do command more money.'

'Don't insult me!'

'Let me assure you,' he released her and walked away,

'offering you higher pay is not an insult but a necessity. You must dress the part, as you would any other. You're the fiancée of a prominent man, a rich man, one day to be a titled man. You can't go about in patched jeans and ancient sweater.'

'I shall dress how I like!' She knew she was behaving like a child, but she was determined to go down – she was forced to acknowledge that she was going down – fighting.

'But you won't, my sweet. From now on, until our "engagement" ends, you'll dress as *I* like. And I like my wife-to-be to be well dressed.'

'I'm not your wife-to-be and you know it!'

'For the moment you are. You can't complain, you started it.'

Should she say, 'No, your brother started it'? What would Alaric say to that – that she was unscrupulous in trying to shield herself from the consequences by incriminating an innocent man? I'm sorry, Mr. Stoddart, I can't go through with it. I can't act a lie—'

'There's no lie about it. It's a fact. You must go through with it. Look.' He showed her half a dozen newspapers with her photograph – the one in the Stoddart dress – followed by the announcement of her engagement to Mr. Alaric Stoddart.

'I'm sorry. You'll have to release me. If you don't, I'll tell the newspapers they've been wrongly informed. I'll—'

He gripped her shoulders, shaking her. 'You'll do no such thing, my girl.' He removed his hands. 'And even if you did, I should immediately refute your denial, saying we'd had a lovers' quarrel which had now been resolved. I'm not releasing you—' He stopped and said, smiling, 'Except on one condition.'

She asked faintly, 'What condition?'

'If you get yourself an acting job, a part – a good part in a play, I'll let you go.'

Her cheeks burned. 'You know that's a virtual impossibility. I haven't had even a small part for months . . .'

He shrugged. 'That's my condition. Otherwise, you

remain my fiancée for as long as I need you to play the part of my fiancée.' He went to the door. 'A ring is called for.'

She was appalled. 'I can't wear your ring.'

'No? Then whose ring are you going to wear – Jay's?'

He led the way along the Dress Corridor – the pearl-studded gown was back on the stand – and stopped in front of a carefully secured display case. From his pocket he took a bulky set of keys, selected one and opened the case. His hand reached inside and unlocked an inner case from which he withdrew a gold ring. The large trans-lucent, red-stained opal glistened in a setting of diamonds and cultured pearls.

He closed the cases, locking each one.

'Give me your engagement finger.'

Reluctance and a strong sense of unreality held her left hand to her side. He repeated his command and she found herself obeying. He slipped the ring on to her finger. 'That ring,' he said, still holding her hand, 'has great value, both sentimental and financial. I trust you to take care of it.'

'I know. I've often told visitors that it's worn by the chosen partners of the heirs to Underlings.' She looked at the ring, her colour deepening because he had seen fit to remind her of the need to care for it. 'Don't worry, Mr. Stoddart,' she said bitterly, 'I won't run away with it and sell it to a dealer and keep the money.'

'You'd better not.' He smiled mockingly. 'And the name's Alaric, *darling*.'

'I now pronounce you,' said a voice behind them, 'man and his mate.'

Petra, pulling her hand from Alaric, swung round. 'Jay! How could—'

He cut off her words with a kiss, then grinned defiantly at his brother. 'Congratulations, Alaric – and thanks for stealing my girl.'

'Mr. Stoddart!' Alaric's secretary called from the end of the corridor. 'Phone call. There have been so many people wanting to congratulate you, but I've told them all you were too busy to speak to them. This one's from London, from – from,' she looked doubtfully at Petra, 'Lady Yvette. She insists on speaking to you.'

'I'll bet she does!' jeered Jay.

Alaric gave him a crushing look and left them. He called over his shoulder, 'Take today off, Petra. I'll contact Mr. Winters. He'll deputize.

'Oh, but Mr. – I mean Alaric, I'd rather—'

'You heard what I said. I'll see you later.'

It was then that her changed status and relationship with the master of the house hit her squarely. 'Jay,' she said, 'how *could* you!'

'Shush ... Come in here, sweetie.' He opened a door marked 'Private' – it was a small room used by the cleaners – and pulled her inside.

'Why did you do it, Jay?' she asked. 'He blamed me, accused me of all sorts of awful things ...'

'But didn't you tell him you had nothing to do with it?'

'I tried to, but he didn't believe me. He was so angry, Jay. I told him to deny the story. Instead, he made it official, told the whole world. I think it was his way of getting his own back, of hurting me ...' She had difficulty in controlling the tears.

'Don't take it to heart, Pet. Jenny and I meant it partly as a joke, and partly – well, we hate his wonderful Yvette. What better way to get her out of his life than this?'

'But didn't it occur to you that it might backfire? He now thinks I'm grasping and unscrupulous and—'

'I'll tell him the truth, Pet.' He kissed her cheek. 'Don't worry about it. Must go, the hordes are hammering at the gates. Take it easy today. I'll come across and see you this evening.'

'I'll be here, Jay. He's having me moved to the main guest room.'

Jay whistled. 'He's really doing the thing properly. That, incidentally,' he said from the door, 'is where his precious Yvette resides when she comes to visit him. When she knows she's been ousted from what she's come to regard as her private property – let alone her private man – will there be trouble!'

They went into the corridor and Mrs. Carr, Alaric's secretary called, 'Miss Bain, phone for you.' As Petra approached she said, 'In Mr. Stoddart's office, Miss Bain.'

Alaric was smiling as he spoke to the caller, but broke off to say, 'Here she is now.' He held out the receiver. 'Your mother.'

Petra put a hand to her throat. 'My mother?'

He frowned. 'Surely you want to speak to her?'

'But what shall I tell her? I can't let her go on believing . . . I'll tell her the truth.' She seized the receiver and said, 'Mum, how lovely to hear . . . Yes, I know, but . . . Thanks, Mum – and Dad, but it's not—' Petra closed her eyes. 'Yes, it's wonderful, but—' She sighed. 'Did you? In the paper?' She turned from Alaric and leaned with her back against the desk. 'Yes, he is – nice. The ring? It's beautiful. Look, Mum, I'll write. The wedding?' She clenched her fist. 'We – we haven't decided – yet. Of *course* I'll tell you in good time. Goodbye, Mum – both of you.' Alaric took the receiver from her shaking fingers.

Petra stood silent, head down, hands clutching the desk behind her, fighting for control.

'So you didn't tell her the truth?'

'How could I? She was so excited, so pleased, so happy for me, for us . . .' She rounded on him. 'How *could* you? Now do you see what you've done?'

'What *I've* done? Aren't you standing truth on its head? Shouldn't it be what *you've* done? You, who made the "announcement" in the first place? You, who got us "engaged"?'

'But you needn't have carried through the lie, you needn't have told the world.'

'So you admit you were responsible?'

Petra realized that what she had just said could, if wrongly interpreted, be called an 'admission of guilt'. She shrugged. What was the use of denying it?

'I've fixed the date of the engagement party.'

'*Party?*' she cried. 'But the whole thing's a sham. How can we celebrate something which both you and I know is untrue?'

'But, my love,' his voice was mocking and she flinched – how could he desecrate such a tender expression? – 'it is *not* a sham, and it *is* true. We are engaged – until we become dis-engaged. We're not playing at an engagement. I warned you you'd have to take all the consequences of your action and one of them is an engagement party. You are my fiancée.' He spoke each word clearly. 'In the eyes of the world you are going to be my wife, you're going to become Mrs. Alaric Stoddart. You can recoil from the fact as much as you like, but my dear girl, you put your head in the noose. Can I be blamed if I pull tighter and tighter until you choke?'

The phone rang. 'Who? Lord Fellowes? Put him through. Mortimer? Thanks, man. Yes, it was sudden and quick. I didn't want any other wolf to get his teeth into her! She's here with me.' He flicked his eyes over her. 'Her beauty defies description. You'll have to wait until you see her. Come to the engagement party. And Meg. You'll get an invitation. Speak to the lady? Why not?' He beckoned. 'Petra?' She shrank away. He put his hand over the mouthpiece. 'Come on, girl. Act, act for all you're worth.'

Petra shook her head, terrified, but took the receiver. 'L-Lord Fellowes? Oh, thank you, M-Mortimer.' She laughed. 'Yes, he's – he's wonderful. How – how did I do it? Well, I just looked at him and – yes, that was enough! I – I'll look forward to meeting you, too.' She handed over to Alaric who listened and said to his friend,

'Shy?' He looked at her. 'Perhaps. How did I manage to catch her? The old Stoddart magnetism! Yvette?' His voice hardened. 'Took it badly. But I—' He glanced at Petra. 'But I was able to pacify her. Two women at once? No, man, not even a Stoddart can run to that!'

Petra ran to the door. He snapped, 'Come back here! Sorry, Mortimer, a little domestic misunderstanding. I'm bringing my future wife to heel.' There was laughter from the other end and the conversation was over.

'What's the matter?' Alaric asked narrowly. 'Jealous?'

'I've had,' she answered, her voice shaking, 'as much as

124

I can take. I'm going. I'm leaving. I'm returning to London, to – to normality.'

'To poverty? To skimping and scraping and the shake of the head when you ask for a job?'

'What of it? I'm used to that sort of environment. It's real. it's sincere, it's straightforward and unpretentious. I'm just – just not made for your sort of life, the high society you move in. My parents aren't rich, but so what? That's nothing to be ashamed of. And at least I'd be out of this atmosphere, this acting a lie– the lie that you love me, the lie that I – that I – love you.'

'Tell me something. Have you discovered the state of your feelings at last?'

Had he guessed her secret? 'What – what do you mean?'

'Have you realized after all that you love my brother? Is that what you're trying to say?'

'I told you, I'm – fond of Jay.'

'*Fond*? Is that the only word you know to express deep emotion? Don't you know the meaning of the word *love*?'

She stared at him. If she were to tell him just how the love she felt at that moment hurt like the plunge of a knife under her ribs . . .

'Perhaps,' he went on, 'you're more familiar with the emotion of hate? You hate me, is that it?'

'No, I—' she was a stranger to prevarication, 'I – I don't hate—' How could she finish the sentence? What would he infer from it – the opposite, that she loved him? She sat in a chair near the door. 'Please leave me alone. Stop your inquisition.'

'Petra?' She raised her head. 'I'm sorry, but we'll have to call a truce. For the moment, I—' what he was going to say seemed to be costing him some effort, 'I need you. We shall have to see this thing through – together. I'll let you go all in good time. Then you can marry Jay or any other man you fancy. Just play along with me for a while.'

It took her some time to answer, but at last she whispered, 'I'll stay.'

'Thanks.' He drew out his cheque book.

'I don't *want* any money!'

'It's part of the bargain. I'm giving you a cheque – a blank cheque – to buy clothes. It's essential, I'm afraid. Clothes to fill the wardrobes, dresses not only for the engagement party but for the invitations we'll receive.'

She was horrified at how deeply she was becoming involved with his way of life. 'Must I?'

'Regard the clothes as stage props. Have tomorrow off. Mr. Winters will deputize again. Take Jenny with you. She knows the best shops.'

Petra took the cheque. 'You're very kind.'

He smiled. 'Not kind – practical. A realist, if you like.'

'Alaric?' He raised his eyebrows. 'Do I have to move into the main guest room?'

'You'd prefer to remain in the coach house?' She nodded. He considered the matter but shook his head. 'It would look bad. As my fiancée, whether it's true or not, you would be expected to want to be near me.' He smiled at her disappointment. 'It's not for ever.' He looked at his watch, dismissing her. 'You'll probably find them moving your stuff over here now.' He touched her cheek with a careless finger. 'Take heart. Jay's around. He'll help you through your – ordeal. While you're living here, just look on Underlings as a top-class hotel, the kind in which we shared a room not so long ago. Remember?'

She coloured at the memory. She had been after 'marriage and money', he had asserted. Had he now proved, to his satisfaction, that he was right?

CHAPTER EIGHT

By evening, Petra was installed in her new living quarters. 'Guest room', she discovered, was a misnomer. It was a suite of rooms, each of palatial size, consisting of a bedroom with a small dressing room leading off it, a living-room and a bathroom.

The bed was a four-poster and canopied and draped with curtains. The moulded and painted ceiling was a mass of brilliantly conceived, hopelessly intertwined angelic-looking figures. Paintings covered the walls and over the silver fireplace was an elaborately-framed mirror.

In the living-room were tapestry-covered chairs and antique furniture. Despite the landscapes and portraits which gazed down upon her, Petra preferred the more modest living-room to the overwhelming bedroom, where the past almost tangibly sprang to life, where the ceiling, painted though it was by a genius, depressed, because the scenes it represented were too vivid for her lively imagination to bear.

It was in the living-room that Jay found her, sitting primly on a chair, hands clasped, hardly daring to breathe, and as out of place as a buttercup at a flower show. He laughed at the sight of her, mentally huddled into a corner, but bravely trying to fit herself into the ornate surroundings.

'Oh, Jay,' her lip trembled, 'I think I'd rather be in digs in an attic room with a window that won't open, or in my parents' cottage, than this. I don't think I can stand it for long.'

He drew up a chair beside her. 'I'm really sorry to have inflicted this on you, Pet.' He took her hand. 'I told Alaric it was all my fault.' He played with her fingers. 'Sorry to say, he didn't believe me. Said I was only saying it to protect you. He said in any case, it was irrelevant who was to blame now. You two were engaged, no matter how short a time it might last. To him it's a real engagement, even though in six months' time it might be officially broken off.'

'But, Jay, he's even going to have an engagement party, asking all his friends, lords and ladies and business associates. He told me to make it the acting role of my life.'

'M'm. That's something you'll discover as you get to know him. He's hard, he's callous and he's not easily deflected from a set course.'

'I've no intention of "getting to know" him, Jay.'

Jay walked about, kicking at the tufts of the priceless carpet. 'I think he has other ideas, Pet.'

'Jay,' she said, her eyes filling, 'why did you do it?'

He pulled her up and held her head against his shoulder. 'Shall I tell you why? Because I thought you were in love with him.' She stiffened in his arms. 'Because the night we shared your couch in the coach house and you went to sleep, you kept muttering his name over and over again.'

So in her dreams she had given herself away. She had to find an explanation. 'But the night Alaric and I spent in the car, he told me that when I woke up I spoke your name. From which he deduced all sorts of things, all of them wrong. So you see, it doesn't follow that because I spoke his name in my sleep I was in love with him, any more than it followed that because I said "Jay" when he was with me, I was in love with—' She stopped, horrified at how she might be hurting his feelings.

'All right, I get the message, Pet.' He held her close. 'You don't love him, you don't love me. There's no man been lucky enough yet to break through your barriers.'

Jay began to put her from him, but she clung. He was the only familiar landmark in the wilderness in which she was wandering. As long as he was there, she felt she could see it through. She didn't love him, but she was fond of him, however much Alaric ridiculed the word.

The door opened and they pulled apart. 'Don't break it up,' he grated, 'I'm only looking for my fiancée. I'm broad-minded. I don't mind finding her in another man's arms – as long as she reciprocates and doesn't object to finding me in another woman's arms.'

'Calm down, brother,' said Jay, on his way to the door. 'She's just told me she doesn't love me any more than she loves you.' He left them.

Petra sat down, bracing herself to take what she feared was coming, but all Alaric said was, 'You're pale. Are you ill?' She shook her head. He approached and tipped up her chin. 'When did you last eat?' She was silent. 'Did you have lunch?' She shook her head. 'Why not?'

'I couldn't face food.'

He threw her chin away. 'Are you mad? What is this ridiculous habit you have of starving yourself?'

'My way of life until I came here conditioned me to doing without. And not only food.'

'Then it's a habit you'll change forthwith. While you're here under my roof as my wife-to-be, you're my responsibility. Whatever you want, whatever you need is yours for the asking. Do you understand?'

You're wrong, she wanted to say, there's one thing I can't have and never will. Your love. But she nodded.

'You're also dining with us tonight and every night. Mrs. Osborn is serving dinner now.'

Jenny and Jay were waiting when they arrived. Jenny embraced her, whispering, 'Sorry, Pet. We honestly didn't mean to inflict the entire works on you. Cheer up. It won't be for long.'

The meal was a strain. If it hadn't been for Jenny's continuous chatter, the atmosphere would have been intolerable. She promised to go with Petra next day to select a wardrobe of clothes. 'Leave it all to Aunt Jenny. We'll patronize the best shops and you can act snooty because you're Alaric's fiancée.'

'It's more likely,' said Jay, 'knowing Petra as I do,' he threw a quick, spiteful look at his brother, 'that she'll end up saying "Yes, madam," "No, madam" to the sales lady!'

After coffee, Jay and Jenny melted away and Alaric invited Petra into his private drawing-room. There was no way out of the invitation. 'Care to hear some music? I'm a classical addict. What are your tastes?'

'Similar. But I never listen. My transistor radio's so inferior the music sounds terrible and I have no record player.'

'Then listen now. My equipment's the best.' He smiled, mocking her, 'I only ever buy myself the best.'

Meaning, she thought, that he had bought her. But, she told herself, one thing I do know, I'm not the best.

As he put a record on the turntable he asked, 'Feeling better now you've been fed?'

'Yes, thank you.' The conversation was so impersonal they might have been members of a music society.

He indicated that she should sit on the couch. He sat beside her. She clasped her hands, holding herself taut, but as the music had its way she forgot how near he was, she forgot the emotions his magnetism aroused and revelled instead in the profound feelings the music evoked. When he took her hand, moving it between them and covering it with his, she tolerated his touch, knowing she had no alternative. If he had chosen to make passionate love to her she could not have repelled him. As her fiancé he had every right.

The music made the feel of him less difficult to bear. She relaxed, her head drooping back to a satin-covered cushion. She imagined that he loved her as she loved him, that they were really going to be man and wife – that they would live in a modest house near a town and he would go to work every morning, like all the neighbours' husbands and return to her and the children every evening . . .

'Petra? You've drifted away. Where to?'

'Nowhere that you can follow.'

He thrust her hand away and turned off the record player. 'You look tired. You'd better go to bed.'

'I am tired.' From the door she said 'Goodnight, Alaric.'

'Goodnight,' he answered, with his back to her.

Petra braved the dark magnificence of the bedroom. She undressed and folded her clothes, taking her time about it. It was such an everyday, pleasantly normal thing to do in such overwhelming surroundings. The bath she had refreshed rather than relaxed her, stimulated rather than soothed. She wandered about, wrapping her housecoat round her irritatingly lively body, returning to the living-room, back into the bedroom and then into the dressing-room, with its unmade-up single divan bed against the wall. There was a door, but it was locked. She supposed it was a cupboard the cleaners used – most of the rooms seemed to have one.

At last, weary with trying to make herself tired, she climbed – really climbed – into bed. But her eyes remained obstinately open. The canopy, even though she could hardly see it, worried her; the curtains and posts worried her too, and when, groping for the switch, she turned on the bedside light, the mass of painted figures writhing on the ceiling came to life and terrified her.

She dropped down from the high bed and went to the window. She opened it, but the draught and the sighing darkness made her shiver, so she shut it out and drew the curtains across. It was no use, she could not sleep in that room. The dressing-room – there was a bed in there, wasn't there?

In desperation she dragged an armful of covers from the four-poster bed and trailed them towards the smaller room. Her foot caught in the flex of the bedside lamp and she tripped, bringing the lamp crashing to the floor. She plunged on in the pitch darkness, feeling the prick of broken glass pressing into her foot. She limped the rest of the way to the dressing-room and sat, clutching the bedclothes, on the nearest available support, which happened to be the bed. She was wrapped around with darkness and a terror such as she had not experienced since childhood.

A key turned, the door she had dismissed as cupboard came open. Beyond it was dimmed lighting. Filling the doorway was Alaric Stoddart, a half-length blue quilted dressing-gown over his pyjama trousers. So it was a communicating door to his apartment, the door through which, when Yvette was his guest, he no doubt came and went at all times.

'What, in heaven's name, is the matter with you?'

She held the trailing bedclothes as if they were a giant teddy bear. 'That room,' she breathed, 'it frightens me. I can't sleep in it, I'm sorry.' She shivered. 'The paintings on the ceiling, the roof over the bed . . .'

'Too much imagination. Only to be expected of an actress, I suppose.' So, with contempt, he dismissed the vital ingredient that made all actors tick. 'What was the crash?'

'The lamp. I've broken the bedside lamp – I tripped over the flex. I'm sorry. I'll pay.'

He switched on the light and stared at the carpet. 'Blood. You've hurt yourself?'

'My foot. I think I trod on some glass.'

He tutted. 'Let me look.' He removed the bedclothes from her arms and she hugged herself, conscious of the inadequacy of her nightdress. He looked her over swiftly and lifted up her foot. 'I'll get some water. This needs bathing.' He rooted in his pocket, produced a clean folded handkerchief and rested her foot on it. He returned to his room and after a few moments came back with an earthenware basin and a roll of cotton wool. Gently he cleansed her foot of chips of glass and covered the wound with plaster. His touch excited her and her voice was a whisper as she thanked him. He held her eyes, her large, tired eyes, and asked, 'Where are your slippers?'

She nodded towards the bedroom like a child indicating a dark cellar into which it wouldn't dare to venture. He switched on the light and went in, returning with a pair of pink mules, which he slipped on to her feet. Again she thanked him and he said, 'Just call me Prince Charming, Cinderella.'

She gave a weak smile and thanked him again, expecting him to leave, but he told her to stand up while he made the divan into a bed for her to sleep in.

'I'll do it,' she protested, 'you can't make my bed.'

'My sweet,' he drawled, 'I can make you what I like. As your fiancé, I can not only make your bed, I could if I wished share it with you.'

She stared. 'You wouldn't!'

His hands found his pockets and he contemplated her flushed face, wide eyes, parted lips. 'Are you challenging a Stoddart?'

'No, no.' She backed away. He bent down and tucked in the sheets and blankets while Petra helped on the other side.

'Get in.'

'When you've gone.'

'So shy with me, yet so free with my brother?'

She thought that if she thanked him yet again for his attentions he might go, but instead of leaving her, his arms went round her. She tipped back her head to look into his face. What, oh, what did he want of her? He kissed her tenderly, gently, and to her dismay the fear she had felt earlier when she had been alone in that dark room caught up with her. She found herself clinging to him as she had clung to Jay, but with what a difference, with what a terrifying rush of feeling!

His kiss changed and she felt fear of another kind. What was he thinking of her now – that she was trying to coerce him into marrying her after all by allowing him, inviting him to anticipate marriage? She struggled out of his arms and stood panting, looking up at him. 'I'm sorry,' she whispered. 'It – it was the little girl in me coming out.'

'I'm aware of that, my sweet. Don't fool yourself that I thought anything else.' He held up the key. 'I'll leave it on your side of the door.' He pushed it into the keyhole. 'If you need me again, come in to me. Wake me if I'm asleep. Lock the door or not, as you wish. Goodnight.'

As he closed the door behind him, she turned the key.

Petra and Jenny returned from shopping with boxes full of clothes. After only an hour, Petra had wanted to stop, but Jenny had urged her on. 'It's not your money. You're doing my brother a favour by agreeing to stay engaged to him. Take advantage of everything he offers.'

Petra wished she could tell her that Alaric thought so badly of her already that if she did just that it would support his conviction that she wanted only his money and his name.

Alaric, when they met at dinner, showed little interest. It was Jay who asked the questions. 'Did you play the great lady?' he wanted to know. 'Or did you sit shaking in a corner and put yourself at the mercy of the superior sales ladies?'

Jenny laughed, saying, '*I* put them in their place. If I hadn't been there, I think Petra would have taken fright and left empty-handed.'

Alaric was silent and Petra wondered if he was even listening to the chatter, but when Jay said, 'I shall demand a dress show given by the world-shattering model, Petra Bain,' Alaric came to life.

'If anyone here is entitled to make demands on Petra, it's I, not you, brother. Remember that.'

Jay subsided under the snub and Jenny made a face behind her hand. After coffee, in Alaric's private room, Petra said, a little timidly, 'I thought you would want to see what I spent your money on.'

'Not my money, yours. I gave it to you.'

She said quietly, 'When I go, I'll leave the clothes behind.'

He appeared not to notice. 'Did you choose a dress for the engagement party?'

'Yes,' eagerly, 'do you want to see it?'

'No. Sit down.' She obeyed, but not next to him. She chose a striped, satin-covered upright chair. 'The invitations for the party are being printed and will be ready in a couple of days. I've fixed it to take place in ten days' time. Are you agreeable?' She nodded. 'I'd like a list of your friends and relatives so that invitations can be sent to them.'

She was aghast that he was taking it so seriously. 'You expect me to act a lie in front of my relatives?'

He said coldly, 'Do I have to repeat that this is not a lie? This is a real engagement, there's no pretence. That it will eventually be broken off has no bearing on the fact that at present,' he spoke clearly, 'you are my wife-to-be.' He stood in front of the fireplace, with his back to its carved overmantel. 'Is that understood? Now,' he searched in his pocket and handed her a notebook and pen. 'Your list of guests.'

She took them, shaking her head. 'You probably won't believe me, but I don't make friends easily. I've moved around a lot and it takes me all my time to make some sort of living, let alone looking for acting jobs. So you see, I haven't got any friends except—' she sighed, 'Jay. And now Jenny.'

She handed back the things he had given her. 'Relatives? Your parents, at least. They can stay here. They'll be given every comfort, every possible attention.'

She could not look at him. 'You're very kind, but I couldn't subject them to such – such deceit.' She raised her eyes. 'I happen to love my parents. I can't pretend to their faces something that patently isn't true. It's one thing misleading them at a distance, another simulating happiness and – and joy when they're here to see me. They know me too well, they'd see there was something wrong. As it is they're going to be terribly disappointed when they eventually learn the truth.'

'I see.' He turned towards the fire. 'I shall inform my father of the party, but he won't come.' A pause, then, 'You'd have no objections, I take it, if I invited Yvette?'

Petra took a breath and forced herself to say, brightly, 'Your girl-friend? Why should I object? After all,' she stood, clasping her hands, 'my boy-friend will be here, won't he?' She ran from the room.

Petra abandoned all attempt to reconcile herself to the main bedroom. Sleep, she knew, would not come to her there. If it did, it would be interlaced with nightmares of writhing figures threatening to smother her. She had turned out the light in the dressing-room and was settling down in bed when the handle of the communicating door turned.

A voice said, 'Let me in, Petra.' She half-sat up. The key was on her side. But she knew that, in spite of the fact that he had in effect given her the power to say 'no', the key might just as well be on his side. It was impossible to refuse entry to the master of the house, especially when he was – however temporarily – her future husband. In any case, it had not been a request, but a command.

The key grated, her heart pounded, her eyes lifted agitatedly to his. As his gaze wandered over her she wished she had put on her wrap before diving across the room to unlock the door. 'So you're still sleeping in here? You find the double bed too big? Too cold? Too lonely?' She stayed silent, letting his baiting pass. 'That could be remedied,' he persisted.

She lifted a pale, rebellious face to his. 'What do you want?'

'Don't ask me that. I might tell you.' She looked away from his mocking smile. He leaned against the door frame, arms folded across his dressing-gown. 'I would have spoken to you earlier about the engagement party arrangements, but your rather theatrical exit earlier this evening brought an abrupt end to our conversation. May I continue from where we left off? You may or may not know that I have a large circle of acquaintances. There will consequently be a great assortment of people at the party, among them a number from the so-called "top stratum". I'm aware of your aversion to such people. May I assume that you'll hide that aversion for the duration of their visit, that you'll be as pleasant to them as you'll no doubt be to the humble villagers and domestic staff who will also be present?'

'What do you take me for?' she blazed. 'A moron? An ill-mannered, untutored ignoramus?'

He walked across to her and pulled her against him. He seemed amused. 'With such a vocabulary at your command, you're anything but untutored and ignorant. I apologize. Am I forgiven?' He tilted her chin and looked into her stormy eyes. She closed them and he laughed. She could not hold his gaze. He had turned on the charm which flooded through her like the sudden warmth of the sun on a blustery day. His lips brushed hers and settled and she held her breath, but he let her go and returned to the door.

'Have I your consent to give the go-ahead to the catering firm I'm employing? They'll handle all the arrangements and anything they don't cover, Mrs. Osborn will take over, with the help from other members of the domestic staff.'

'Which means it will be entirely out of my hands?'

'Yes. Does it worry you? If it does, I'll cancel my instructions and let you take over.'

'No, thanks. I have no experience whatsoever of such activities. I'd only make a mess of it. It's as well I'm not really going to be your wife. You'd find me hopeless where entertaining is concerned, especially the élite.'

'I scent a touch of sarcasm. All the same, I think you're underestimating yourself.'

'Thanks for saying that, but I'm being honest, not modest.' Tiredness and misery were driving her on. 'I'm not your sort at all. I don't speak your language. Jay's language, yes, but not yours. Jay understands my background, Jay understands how I feel . . .'

'Jay's a paragon,' he snarled, 'Jay's perfection, Jay's faultless. *So why don't you marry him?*'

She covered her face. 'Because I don't love him,' she whispered, but Alaric had gone.

When Petra saw Jay next morning he told her Alaric had left for London. 'Didn't he tell you?'

Petra sighed. 'No. We parted last night on rather bad terms.'

'He didn't try anything on? I mean—'

'No, but even if he did, as his fiancée there would be little I could do about it.'

'Look, Pet, you're my—'

'I'm not your girl any more, Jay.' Petra's eyes filled and she turned away. 'I'm sorry.'

'Pet, you don't love the man?'

She asked, side-stepping the question, 'Will he be meeting Yvette in town?'

'Almost a certainty. By the way, before he went he said if you don't want to work today, or any other day, you needn't.'

'Of course I'll work. I can't sit around and get paid for doing nothing.'

So Petra showed the crowds round Underlings again. Word must have got about that not only were the owner's younger son and daughter acting as guides but the bride-to-be of the elder Stoddart son, too. Some of the visitors asked outright if she was the young lady soon to be married to the heir to the estate, and when she told them shyly that she was engaged to him – a difference so subtle they could not detect it – they took photographs of her by flashlight.

There was no word from Alaric. The preparations for the party rose to a climax. Mrs. Osborn consulted Petra frequently, but she was afraid to give directions in case she went against Alaric's wishes. In the end she suggested to the housekeeper that she should phone Mr. Stoddart at his suite of rooms in London.

One evening, four days before the party, Mrs. Osborn took her advice. Then she called Petra. 'Mr. Stoddart wishes to speak to you, Miss Bain. Will you take the call in his office?'

Petra picked up the phone. 'This is Petra. Did you want to speak to me?'

Softly he replied, 'Yes, darling. How are you?'

Why couldn't she tell him the truth? He was her fiancé, after all. Why couldn't she say 'I wish you'd come home. I love you very much and I'm longing to see you again'? 'I'm well, thank you.'

'How are things going?'

'I'm – I'm floundering a bit. I'm sorry, but I did warn you. I wish . . .'

'You wish – ?'

'It doesn't matter.'

A pause, then, 'Missing me?'

Another pause. 'Yes,' she whispered.

'Do you know,' came the mocking response, 'I've half a mind to believe you.' Then, whispering, 'Goodnight, sweet.'

The charm was coming through. It was sweeping her off her feet like a great tidal wave. 'Goodnight, Alaric.'

'Darling,' his voice insisted.

She echoed, in a murmur, 'Darling.'

It was two days to the party. There was a bustle and commotion in the drive. The master of the house had come home. Petra stood uncertainly at the top of the main staircase, looking down on the entrance hall. She was wearing a clinging scarlet jersey dress which she had bought with Alaric's money.

She was apprehensive yet excited, elated but afraid. How would they greet each other? With the restraint which had marked their relationship so far, or the joy of lovers reunited?

The swing doors were held open. Cases were carried in. Petra counted up to eight and stopped. They could not all belong to Alaric. Following the cases was a tall, slim young woman, auburn-haired, aristocratic, beautiful. Every movement revealed self-knowledge. She knew she possessed grace and poise, she was aware that her dress sense was faultless and that her clothes were draped on her swaying body with such elegance that it was as though they could speak of their perfection. It was, Petra knew, Lady Yvette Duffey.

Behind her, with the weariness of a long drive shadowing his features, came Alaric. His eyes lifted and the sight of Petra seemed to switch on a light in his face. He put down the cases he was carrying, strode past his astonished companion and sprinted up the carpeted stairs. Under the archway above the great staircase he took Petra into his arms, kissing her long and tenderly.

His lips touched her ear and he murmured, 'Act for all you're worth. Don't let me down, Pet.'

'Pet' he had called her, Jay's and Jenny's name. A mistake? No, the Stoddart charm turned on, this time for his girl-friend's benefit. It was a dress rehearsal for what was to come – the show of love over the period of the engagement party when guests by the dozen would be arriving at Underlings.

So Petra had to 'act for all she was worth', she had to tell the world how much she loved Alaric Stoddart, even though she could not tell her love to him.

She nodded, her eyes shining as she knew he would wish them to, and she dared to reach up and kiss him. He held her by the waist and searched her face, then led her by the hand down the stairs to the great hall.

'Petra darling, this is Yvette, Yvette Duffey, a friend of mine.'

At the description the doe-eyes grew waspish and turned on the man she apparently considered her own. But the eyes, where the recipient was concerned, seemed to have lost their sting. He did not even flinch.

'Yvette, my fiancée, Petra Bain.'

The eyes settled on Petra, whose body held no antidote to the poison. She winced under the injection of animosity from that gaze, and instinctively pressed nearer to the man beside her. He felt her recoil and his arm drew her close.

She looked up at him spontaneously, intending to apologize, then remembered the role she was playing. Her smile met his, his lips were not far behind and touched hers. He was, Petra decided, trying to still her pounding heart, a better actor than Jay.

'Alaric,' said the tight-lipped onlooker, 'has told me all about you, Miss Bain.' The words were commonplace, the tone vitriolic. Miss Bain, congratulating herself on her improved acting technique, inclined her head with a grace worthy of the aristocracy.

'You have the advantage of me, then, Lady Yvette. I wish he had returned the compliment and told me about you, then we would have been on equal terms.' She looked up at Alaric again. 'Perhaps I can persuade him to talk about you some time, when we're alone.' The smile she gave him was over-sweet, like a cup of tea with too much sugar in it.

He gave her a sly look, as if guessing her tactics. 'Remind me to *talk* some time, darling, when we're alone.' She coloured at his meaning, in spite of herself. He gave her a playful pat as if dismissing her into the role of the employee and she slipped back involuntarily into the role of the employee. As she climbed the stairs she heard Yvette say, 'Tell them to take my cases to my room, Alaric. If I don't have a shower at once, I shall melt!'

'Mrs. Osborn,' Alaric called to his housekeeper who

had been hovering, 'Lady Yvette's cases to the second guest room, please.'

'Second?' came the furious question. 'The *main* guest room, Alaric. That's mine, darling, the one I always have.' Her voice became silky. 'Next to yours, darling.'

'Sorry, Yvette, it's occupied. My fiancée has it.'

Petra turned. 'Alaric, if Lady Yvette wants it for herself, I don't mind. I'll move out. You know I don't like—'

'She will have the second guest room.' The words were emphatic and also a dismissal.

Dinner was an uncomfortable affair. Once again Jenny came to the rescue. Her gaiety, her refusal to be abashed by Yvette's superciliousness, eased away the tensions which stretched and intertwined across the table like a delicate web.

Yvette turned to Petra. 'You won't mind, Miss Bain, after you're married to Alaric, sharing him?'

Petra felt like a fly in that web. She struggled to free herself, looked with anguish at her fiancé, but he merely watched her floundering with an enigmatic smile and not a shred of sympathy.

Petra searched for an answer, hoping to find the password which would free her from her verbal entanglement. 'I'm afraid that if you mean with another woman, I'd find it very difficult, if not impossible. On the other hand, if he wanted to go. I'd never hold him against his will. But,' she smiled at her questioner, 'share him? No.'

There was a minor disturbance at the other end of the table, but Petra did not dare meet Alaric's eyes.

'I was thinking,' said Yvette, with cool amusement, 'of his work.'

Petra's cheeks turned scarlet and Alaric burst out laughing. 'Thanks, Yvette,' he said when he had recovered, 'for demonstrating to me indirectly the depth of my future wife's love. You see, she's too shy to tell me to my face.'

The colour stayed in Petra's cheeks. How much was he acting now? And how much had she herself been acting when she had spoken those revealing words?

It was during the evening that Yvette showed how large a claim she had on Alaric Stoddart. Before Petra could reach the couch in Alaric's drawing-room – Jay and Jenny had been invited that evening, too – Yvette had claimed it and pulled Alaric down beside her. He joined her willingly enough, tolerated her arm that had slipped round his and turned his head now and then to admire her attractions. Model that she was, whatever she wore she enhanced, and that evening she had chosen a long dress with a low-cut black velvet top and a brilliant floral-patterned skirt. Beside her, Petra, in her red jersey dress, felt like a gauche office girl.

Yvette talked to Alaric of matters which seemed entirely private to themselves. She discussed his business, their mutual friends, she shifted closer to him and he did not move away.

Jay, sensing the agitation Petra was striving to hide, moved his chair next to hers. Jenny said she felt like a prickly down-to-earth gooseberry in a basket of strawberries and announced that she was going in search of her boy-friend.

She threw a disgusted look at her elder brother to whom Yvette was now clinging, and said that although Martyn might not welcome her with open arms, at least he wouldn't deliberately make up to another woman while she, Jenny, looked on.

Alaric shot a brotherly, if incomprehensible grin in her direction, told her to mind her own business and said he hoped she found her boy-friend in a more tolerant, less anarchistic frame of mind than usual.

'Don't forget,' Alaric said as she went to the door, 'to invite him to the engagement party. Although I'm sure he won't come. Think of the aristocracy he'll be forced to mix with.'

'I've already invited him,' Jenny retorted, 'and aristocracy or not, he *is* coming. He likes Petra.' She went out.

'Who doesn't?' said Jay, taking her hand and putting it to his lips in a theatrical gesture. 'Speaking personally, I love Petra.'

He gazed boldly at his brother who turned expressionless eyes towards him. 'Glad to hear it, Jay,' he said evenly. 'It always makes for a good family atmosphere if relatives love one another, especially a brother-in-law and sister-in-law.'

Jay's colour deepened. 'You know damned well—'

'Jay.' Petra's fingers reached out and closed his lips. 'See me to my room? I'm tired.' To Alaric and Yvette, 'Please excuse me. I'm sure you must have a lot to talk about.'

Alaric's eyes narrowed dangerously, but he said, 'Good-night, *darling*. I'll see you later.'

'Please don't bother—' she nearly choked, 'darling. I'll probably be in bed by then.'

'All the better,' said Alaric.

It was Yvette's turn to say with a little pout, 'Darling!'

'Come on,' said Jay, pulling Petra to the door. As they went along the corridor, he said, 'There are times when I could cheerfully throttle my brother. Whose engagement party is this going to be – yours and his or his and Yvette's?'

'You know as well as I do,' Petra told him, 'it's not a real engagement party. He knows it, too. If he wants to make love to Yvette, who am I to stop him? I have no claim on him.'

'Cheer up, Pet.' Jay kissed her lightly. 'A month or so and it'll all be over. You'll both be able to stage a quarrel and everything will be back to normal.'

Petra wished, but doubted, that it would be as simple as that. He left her and she prepared for bed, but feeling alert and, for some reason, apprehensive, she did not settle down at once. Instead, she sat up reading, a bedjacket round her shoulders.

When the summons she had been dreading but not really expecting came, the voice demanded entry not from Alaric's bedroom but from the corridor. Petra replied that she was in bed and about to go to sleep. The answer was that he didn't believe her, and in any case he had a perfect right to come in.

She tiptoed across the floor, turned the key and dived

back into bed. Flushed and panting, she looked up at him defiantly. He closed the door and leaned against it. His jacket was off, his tie removed and his shirt unbuttoned.

'An engaged man has rights,' he said. 'He shouldn't have to go down on his knees to be allowed into the bedroom of the woman he's going to marry.'

'You have no rights. You're not my husband.'

'Yet.'

'You know very well you're never going to be my husband. You know the whole thing's make-believe, a dream ...' She caught her breath, but the slip had not passed him by. He approached her slowly.

'Shouldn't you have said nightmare, darling? A dream implies something desired, longed for ...'

He sat on the bed, an arm went round her shoulders, a hand tipped up her face. Two lips found hers, rested and lifted. She began to panic. 'You've no right to do that, I'm not—'

'But,' he raised her left hand, showed her his ring, 'you are. You're mine, to kiss, to make love to if I wanted. Like this.' He gathered her in his arms, kissed her neck, caressed her. She began to submit, felt her willpower deserting her, made a desperate effort to hold on to it and dug her nails into his shoulder. He sprang away, his eyes blazing. 'You vicious little—'

'What's the matter,' she breathed, her love for him, her frustrated longing playing havoc with her discretion, 'is Yvette listening on the other side of the door? Do you feel it necessary to prove to her as well as to yourself that the ancient virility of the Stoddarts lives on? That she needn't worry because in spite of what you said to Lord Fellowes that you were able to take on only one woman at a time, you're perfectly capable of disposing of two or even more in one night?'

His mouth grew tight, his eyes darkened, His gaze wandered over her, dwelling on her dishevelled state, her sloping shoulders, the whiteness of her throat – and it was there that his hands fastened. 'You provoke me too far and I'll—' His mouth, meaning business, came down –

and a voice from his room called,

'Alaric? Darling?'

He thrust Petra away and she huddled under the bed-clothes. 'Your girl-friend's calling,' she said to the wall, 'don't keep her waiting. You're wasting your time with me. You'll get more out of her, although she doesn't wear your ring – yet. She sat up, pulled at his ring and held it out to him. 'Give it to her. It's not mine. I've no right to it. She's the one you love.'

He took it, gripped her hand and thrust the ring back on to her engagement finger with such force that he drew blood. He opened the communicating door, drew out the key, took it with him and locked the door on his side.

So, Petra thought miserably, turning her tear-damp face to the pillow, his invitation to go in to him whenever she felt the need no longer applied. She wrapped her handkerchief round her aching finger and listened – she was forced to, it was so loud – to the noise which came from Alaric's bedroom. There was laughter and music and the chink of glasses, and Petra felt pangs of jealousy delving so deep inside her it was like a gardener thrusting the prongs of a fork into the soil.

At last there was quiet, which was worse than all the noise they had made, and Petra held her hands to her ears to keep the silence out.

CHAPTER NINE

NEXT morning Yvette kept to her room. Petra was thankful that she did not have to entertain her. She began to dread the two days ahead. If she and Alaric had been really in love, if she had been able to rely on his support, his guidance, his friendship she would not have had a care in the world.

She met him mid-morning outside his room. He was wearing his thick-rimmed spectacles and he looked a stranger. He stopped her as she attempted to pass him without speaking.

'What's the matter? You look pale. Are you ill?'

She avoided his eyes. 'I – didn't sleep well.'

'You'd better rest today.'

'No, thank you. I've no intention of imitating your girl-friend and staying in bed while the rest of the world runs round me doing my bidding, regardless of the nuisance I'm making of myself.'

Her bitterness had got the better of her. He pulled her into his room and closed the door. 'Be careful what you're saying. Sarcasm can arise from wounded feelings. It could imply that you're jealous—'

'Jealous? Me? You must be joking. I don't care how many girl-friends you have. I don't care if you break off this farcical engagement the day after the party. I don't care about anything where you're concerned ...' She drew a breath and was horrified to find a sob jerking at her throat. She covered her eyes and turned away, dismayed that she had broken down in front of him.

Two hands on her shoulders led her to a chair. A drink was pushed into her hand. Alaric sat on the arm of the chair while she sipped the burning liquid. He took the empty glass from her.

'Feeling better? At least it's brought the colour to your cheeks. I take it you've breakfasted?'

'I wasn't hungry.'

He sighed. 'This,' he said, dialling on the internal telephone, 'is where we came in. The first day I met you I fed you and here I am, still feeding you. Mrs. Osborn? Send a tray to my apartment, will you?' My fiancée missed her breakfast and is now consequently almost fainting with hunger, although she won't admit it.' There was respectful laughter from the other end before Alaric rang off.

'You needn't have bothered. I couldn't eat a thing.'

But when the tray arrived, the aroma of the coffee was her undoing. As she ate, Alaric helped himself to a piece of toast and crunched it, watching her do justice to the cook's efforts to tempt her appetite.

Petra said sheepishly, 'I must have been hungry after all.'

He laughed. 'You see, I'm getting to know you. They say the way to a man's heart is through his stomach. I wonder if I kept shovelling a constant stream of food into you, I'd find the way to your heart?'

'You mean feed me as though I were a wild animal in a cage?'

'Wild animal is right.' He felt his shoulder. 'The wound your nails inflicted is still painful. I ought to force you to make amends by kissing it better.'

She turned pink and put the tray from her. 'I'm sorry about that.'

'Oh, don't apologize. I admire a woman with spirit. She presents a challenge to one's masculinity.'

'Which is why, I suppose,' the words came out before she could stop them, 'why you – like Yvette.'

'How you do dwell on Yvette! More than I do, I think.' he patted a cushion. 'Come and sit next to me. Now, give me your hand. For today, and tomorrow and even possibly into the early hours of Wednesday, you and I must call a cease-fire. Perhaps I can reach you better if I explain the set-up in terms of a play. Imagine it, Pet.' He twisted sideways and looked into her face. 'We're an engaged couple. We're madly in love. We can't wait for the day we marry and finally come together. We want to tell the world of our love, to demonstrate it visibly – because that's what this engagement party's all about. And there will be many present who'll be intrigued to meet the woman who has, shall we say, caught Alaric Stoddart at last, Alaric the elusive, Alaric the selective, Alaric the pursuer – and the pursued. I've been called all those names and more before now. Will you behave as though you love me, can't bear to have me out of your sight? When I kiss you will you respond? Will you act the hostess to my friends and acquaintances, make them envious of my fortune in having a girl like you as my future wife?'

He tipped her chin and their eyes held. His charm, his magnetism wrapped about her like loving arms. 'I'll try,' she whispered.

'But it won't be easy?'

'No. But I promise not to let you down.'

'Thanks.' He let her go. 'Only two days, then we can return to fighting each other again.' She laughed and he pulled her up. 'May I kiss you? You won't turn tigress again and rip me to pieces?'

She smiled and he didn't wait for an answer. His lips were gentle and warm and it was as much as she could do to hold her responses in check and prevent her love for him from sweeping in and lifting her off her feet in a terrifying hurricane of feeling.

In the end she had to pull away. He frowned. 'You'll have to do better than that.' He took her into his arms again. 'Perhaps we need another rehearsal?'

But she got away from him. From the safety of the door she asked, 'When the party's over, will you release me from the engagement?'

He became abrupt, his good humour evaporated. 'Impossible. Far too soon. Anyway, you know my condition.'

'But, Alaric—'

He held the door open. 'Keep your promise for the next two days. For the moment, that's all I ask.'

And Petra kept her promise. She had chosen a dress which, she hoped, would please him. It was satin, its colour a glinting gold; the neckline plunged daringly low, and from the waist down wrapped around her body to flow

148

in dramatic, unexpected folds to the floor.

In the State Drawing Room she stood beside Alaric, receiving the guests, the lords and their ladies, local dignitaries, tenants of the Stoddart farms and houses. Staff mingled with the aristocracy, guides, local people, friends of Alaric's friends, Jay's and Jenny's friends; they came without end, bringing their good wishes and their gifts.

Petra smiled, shook hands, laughed, received kisses and compliments on her looks and her cleverness at landing such a big fish as the heir to Underlings. Now and then Alaric's hand felt for hers, holding it for a few moments probably, she thought, to give her extra confidence.

Lord Fellowes, tall, red-faced, jovial – 'Mortimer, please,' he said – introduced his wife, a small, gracious grey-haired smiling woman, and she invited Petra to their residence in London. 'Come and stay any time you're near, my dear, whether Alaric's with you or not.'

In the face of their sincerity, Petra hated the make-believe part she was playing, and hated herself for ever having consented to such deception.

'Alaric,' said Lady Fellowes, 'I congratulate you on your good taste. Such simplicity, such unspoilt sweetness – incredible in this day and age. Mind you keep her that way.' She touched his arm. 'Your girl's delightful.'

Her husband stage-whispered loudly behind his hand, 'Where did you find such a sweetie?'

Alaric laughed and put his arm round Petra's waist. 'You'll never believe me, Mortimer, but she came to me one night in a dream. I touched her and to my joy she was real.'

They laughed. 'A likely tale,' said Mortimer.

Alaric tipped up her face and kissed her. 'Glad you approve of her, both of you, but to tell you the truth,' he smiled wickedly into Petra's eyes, 'she really chose me.'

Mortimer guffawed. 'The temptress, eh? If I'd been you, I wouldn't have needed much tempting. I'd be Adam to her Eve any time!' He passed on his way after his wife.

There was a limitless supply of food, there was wine and there was dancing. Crowds filled the great room, with its priceless paintings, costly carpets, the Chippendale and the Robert Adam furniture pushed to the sides to make room for the dancers. The chandeliers glinted, the candles flickered. Standard lamps and table lamps added their steady glow. At one end of the vast room an orchestra played.

When the dancing began, Alaric led Petra on to the floor. 'Look into my eyes,' Alaric commanded, 'gaze at me as though I'm all you could ever want. If I call you, "Petra, my darling, my beloved," would that help? I'll do anything to encourage you to look as though you love me.' She smiled up at him and her face was radiant with happiness. 'My sweet, that's perfect. You're an actress to your finger-tips. Now I'm going to kiss you. It's part of the bargain, remember.' As his lips rested on hers a light flashed, a camera clicked. 'The press are here, darling, so keep it up. Only a few more hours . . .'

'If,' said Petra, when she could control her voice, 'this is an engagement party, what would a wedding reception be like?'

His eyes mocked her. 'You'll never know, will you?'

Her face fell, she could not help it, and he remonstrated, 'No, no, you mustn't look like that.' He held her face against him to hide its expression from their guests. 'I shall begin to believe you really care.'

Her head came up. 'For your money, of course,' she said.

'If you quarrel with me, I'll spank you. Tonight I shall turn that key, come into your room—'

She put up her hand and covered his mouth. He kissed her fingers. 'Did I remember to tell you,' he said when she allowed him to speak, 'how much I like your dress and how beautiful you look?'

She smiled at him impishly. 'If you're writing this play, you must be more original than that.'

He took a breath. 'The impudence—'

The music stopped, the crowd applauded and Yvette placed herself in front of Alaric. 'Sorry, Miss Bain,' she smiled unpleasantly, 'ex-girl-friend's privilege.'

Petra walked away, hearing, but ignoring, Alaric's

sharp 'Come back!'

Jay's arm went round her. 'Must you look so abominably in love? Must you gaze up at the man as though you adored him?'

She answered wearily, 'It's all part of the act, Jay. He made me promise to pretend. I'm keeping the promise. Only a few hours, he said, and it'll all be over.' Involuntarily, tears sprang to her eyes.

'You mustn't weep in public, sweetie,' Jay said, aghast. 'Turn off that tap, Pet!' Petra smiled and recovered her poise. 'For heaven's sake, Petra, you mustn't fall for the man. He's no more serious about this engagement business than you are. Look at him with that she-cat.'

Alaric was smiling into Yvette's eyes, they were dancing as one. Petra sighed. 'She's beautiful, Jay.' Yvette's dress was filmy and black. The semi-transparent top was demurely fastened at the neck, the rest of it was open to the waist. The skirt touched the floor – but no man looked at the skirt.

'Pet', said Jenny, joining them and overhearing Petra's admiration of the woman Alaric was holding in his arms, 'have you looked at yourself in the mirror? Martyn,' he stood beside her holding her hand, 'isn't Petra stunning? Tell her she's stunning.'

Obediently Martyn told her, but his eyes held admiration.

'Sorry, Martyn,' said Petra, 'to inflict such high society on you today. I appreciate your coming. If it's any consolation,' her eyes swept round the room, 'I – I know how you feel.'

'Misplaced sympathy,' said Jenny. 'He says he's as good as they are, so why shouldn't he mix with the top people?' She gazed up at him as Petra had looked at Alaric before Yvette had taken him away from her. 'But I disagree.'

Martyn frowned. 'So I'm not good enough for you?'

Jenny smiled, reached up and kissed his cheek. 'You're better than they are.'

Martyn smiled into her eyes and they returned to the dancing.

'She's overdoing it,' muttered Jay. 'She chases that man,

but she's wasting her time.'

'*I* think he likes her. No,' she corrected herself, 'I'm sure he loves her.'

'Woman's intuition?' Jay jeered.

'No, woman's observation.'

'If you're so observant, madam, why haven't you seen my signs? Why haven't you noticed the signals I've been flashing to you for months past?'

'Jay, I—'

'Petra.' Alaric was there, pulling her from Jay's arm. 'Dance.'

They were silent as they moved round the room. Alaric was staring into the distance and holding her as though she were just a passing stranger. 'If you don't look at me,' Petra said, 'everyone will think you don't love me, and it would be terrible if they guessed the the truth at our engagement party!'

'You,' he breathed, looking down at her and pressing her to him, 'are a little minx. How dared you walk away from me, when I told you to come back?'

'I had to stand aside when your beautiful girl-friend demanded your attention. After all, I'm not really your—'

His lips, brutal this time, stopped the words. 'Alaric, please ...' Tears threatened again, but she had them under control at once. After a while she said, 'The presents, all those expensive presents, what are you going to do about them when we part?'

'Give them back,' he snapped. 'What else can I do?'

'It's terrible,' she murmured, 'all this pretence—'

'You're letting me down, so kindly shut up.'

'Alaric?' He looked at her. She reached up and kised his cheek as Jenny had done to Martyn. 'You see,' with a provocative smile, 'I can play-act as well as you.'

'You wait,' he breathed, 'until I get you in a dark corner!'

She looked round. 'There aren't any dark corners.'

'If I instructed them to turn the lights down, there would be.' The threat hung tantalizingly on the air.

Half-way through the evening the lights were lowered,

and Alaric did go into a dark corner with Yvette. Petra was looking for him and caught them kissing. She ran from the room into the cold corridor. Jay, who had been watching his brother, followed Petra. He caught her up at the library door.

'Come in here, Pet. No one will find us.' He looked at her face. 'So you're jealous, which means you love him. All right, he's won. I'll tell you something, Petra, if only to set your mind at rest. I watched them. *She* was kissing him.'

'He was letting her do it. He wasn't complaining.'

'Don't look so miserable, Pet. I'll get you a drink.' He was soon back. 'They're dancing together. He watched me leaving with the drinks and looked as though he could poison me.'

'Thought you'd pass the information on to me, I suppose. Let them dance – and kiss. I don't care,' she added viciously.

'Drink up, darling. Here's to your future – may it be successful, may your name go up in lights and may you get the biggest part of your life.' He took her glass. 'Now, since my brother's dallying with another woman on his engagement night, I'll dally with his neglected – and bogus – fiancée.' He kissed her and she tolerated it because of his kindness and his sympathy.

The door opened. 'I've been looking,' said Alaric stiffly, watching them break from each other, 'all over the house.'

'So now you've found us,' said Jay. 'What are you going to do about it? Challenge me to a duel?' He went out.

Petra stood in the centre of the room, hands clasped, waiting for his anger to start. But Alaric gave her a look of contempt, went out and closed the door. She forgot she had seen him kissing Yvette, she forgot she was not really his fiancée. She ran after him, catching him in the corridor. Her hand found his and she tugged his arm to make him stop. 'Alaric?' He would not look at her. 'I'm sorry. Alaric!' She bent his arm and threaded her own through it. 'Please, Alaric!'

He looked down at her, his expression unreadable, left

her arm where it was and led her back to the State Drawing Room. In the doorway he smiled, but it did not reach his eyes. 'We're on stage, *darling*,' he murmured. 'We're the leading players. Keep your promise. It's midnight. Only two more hours and from now until the end, I'm not letting you out of my sight.'

They danced. 'You're wrong. When Yvette says come, you go.'

He raised an eyebrow. 'You wouldn't be jealous?'

'I told you, *no*.'

'Have you eaten this evening? You haven't? I thought I could detect the signs of hunger. Bad temper is one of them. Come with me.' He pulled her to the buffet table. 'Fill – and I mean fill – two plates, please,' he said to the woman helper.

He took the plates, said over his shoulder, 'Follow me,' and Petra trotted obediently behind him all the way to the darkest corner. He told her to sit down, which she did, by the side of a large procelain vase massed with flowers.

He thrust a plate into her hands. 'Eat, woman.'

She ate, avidly, to the last crumb.

'Now,' he took her plate, 'perhaps you'll be more amenable.'

'If,' she said, replete now and provocative, 'this so-called engagement were ever, by a cruel twist of chance, to culminate in marriage, and you were to feed me every time I got bad-tempered, I'd get quite fat.'

'Which,' he said, 'is a poor reflection on your temper. And thanks for your kindly comments on my worth as a husband. "Cruel twist of chance" indeed! Behave yourself and come with me to do the rounds.' He looked at her doubtfully. 'Are you capable of going through the gracious lady routine?'

'What else did I learn at drama school, if not to act?'

'Yes, you learnt the rudiments, at least, as your excellent performance this last day or so as my devoted fiancée has proved. Good enough to please the most critical of audiences.' He pulled her by the hand. 'We'll begin at the other end.'

'I notice,' she said as they walked the length of the room, 'that, in accordance with their comparatively lowly station, all the servants and underlings of Underlings' present master have gathered together all in one place, while the nobility has done likewise in another place.'

'God knows,' he said, under his breath, 'I've tried to make democracy work, I've tried to get them to mingle, but each group has put out a smoke screen and refuses to venture from behind it. What can I do if late twentieth-century equality has failed to reach the outlying villages of England, or penetrated the high-class London establishments of the monied and the titled?'

She warmed to him and said shyly, 'It's good to hear you talk of democracy and equality, Alaric. I didn't believe you thought that way. I'd expect it of Jay, and even Jenny, but not—'

'Not of me?' He stopped her as they reached the dancers and made her face him. 'If you don't deserve to be severely chastised, you young rebel! What exactly do you think I am?'

'Do you really want to know?' She grinned up at him, light-headed with excitement, satisfied appetite and tiredness. 'I think you're arrogant, dictatorial and at times overbearing.'

Instead of smiling, he ground his teeth. 'If it weren't for present company and present circumstances, I'd force you to take back every word of that outrageous statement.'

She thought it wise to apologize and did so. He appeared to be mollified and tugged her towards the group of village people and employees of the estate of Underlings. Petra did not act the gracious lady. She was herself, pleasant and smiling, feeling truly their equal, speaking to them on their own terms, even reminding the girls who worked in the tea room of her brief stay amongst them.

At first they were shy, but they soon lost their reserve and chatted to her as though she were still one of their number – until Alaric, who had been talking to the others, came to claim her.

With the lords and their wives, the knights and their ladies, the County, the businessmen and their associates, it was Petra who was shy. Alaric was on first-name terms with them all, and although he did his best to make Petra feel at her ease – he put his arm round her, pulling her close – he could not get her to relax as she had done with the others.

'If only,' she said, when all the guests had gone and Alaric was walking with her to her room and chiding her for her reticence towards his acquaintances, 'your titled and rich friends had said something intelligent as the villagers did, instead of all that banter and nonsense, I could have conversed with them.'

He laughed shortly. 'So the locals are more intelligent than my highly educated, sophisticated, not to say financially well-endowed friends?'

She knew she was not pleasing him, but at that time of day, in the cold, unfamiliar small hours of the night, with Yvette awaiting her boy-friend's return downstairs, she did not care.

'At least,' she answered defiantly, 'they spoke my language and I theirs. I could talk to them and not feel inferior. Can't you understand I'm not in your class, I'm not your type, I'm not your equal? Why don't you let me go now? I've done my duty, I've kept my promise, I've acted my part . . .'

In the light of the corridor he towered above her, unfamiliar again in his remoteness, his eyes cold, his lips tight and on the verge of anger. 'Please accept my gratitude and thanks for all you've done. But it was your doing in the first place. You put your head in my noose.' He looked reflectively at her throat, his eyes wandered lazily all over her. 'There are two conditions on which I'll free you.'

'*Two* now?'

'Yes, I'm being kind. One condition, as you know, is that you get yourself an acting role with substance, something to prove to the world, as you've proved to me, that you can act.'

'And,' she whispered, 'the other?'

'That you tell me, honestly and unequivocally, that

you're in love with my brother and want to marry him.'

As he walked away, Yvette appeared at the end of the corridor calling his name.

Petra slept until lunchtime and awoke to find a breakfast tray beside her. She pushed it aside. She couldn't face food, anyway. There was too much on her mind. Soon she would have to think about looking for an acting job. This situation couldn't be allowed to drift on indefinitely. Her love for Alaric was dominant in her mind, occupied her waking hours and invaded her dreams.

Now the party was over, the pretence could stop. He need not kiss her again, need not treat her as anything but an employee to be dismissed with the others when the visiting season was over. She couldn't live within sight, sound and touch of the man and yet be denied the expression of her love which, until now, she had been allowed to show under the cover of acting.

She wondered how he would greet her when she saw him again. They had parted on unpleasant terms, which was of course nothing unusual. How would he treat her now there was no necessity for playing at being in love?

When she returned the tray to Mrs. Osborn, she asked whether Lady Yvette was up yet. Mrs. Osborn looked at her with surprise. 'She's gone, Miss Bain, and Mr. Stoddart with her. He's taken her back to London. He said he'd be staying there a while. I thought he might have told you.'

She coloured and said, 'Oh, I – er – expect in the excitement of the party last night he forgot to remind me. He – he did mention something . . .'

The visitors came as usual, the crowds stared and admired and asked questions. Now and then Petra passed Jay or Jenny with their straggling groups of sightseers. They waved discreetly over the bobbing heads.

Petra told herself in the empty days that followed that she mustn't miss Alaric. There would come a time when she would never see him again and she must prepare herself for that. But his face kept coming in front of her as she walked, as she read or looked out over the parkland in the evening sun.

There was no phone call from him. At the end of each day she thought he might contact her if only to ask how she was. He spoke to Jay and occasionally to Jenny, but never asked for her. One evening she was passing through the hall when the telephone rang. She answered and it was Alaric. When he heard who it was, he hesitated, then asked after her health.

'Are you eating?'

'Now and then.'

'When I return, will I find you wasted away because I haven't been there to feed you?'

'Probably. Depends on how long you're away.'

'You're not, by any chance, pining for – anything?'

'No. I just don't feel hungry.'

There was an exasperated sigh, then, 'Is Jay around? Find him for me, will you? But before you go, Petra – I forgot to give you permission to use my apartment whenever you feel inclined. Play some music, read my books. You are, after all, still my fiancée.'

She asked, with seeming innocence, 'How's Yvette?'

There was a brittle silence. 'Get Jay, please.'

Tears rushed to her eyes. 'Yes, *Mr. Stoddart*.'

A· week later he still had not returned. One afternoon there was a phone call from a man calling himself Benedict Reynold. He was an artist, he said, and had been commissioned by Mr. Alaric Stoddart to paint the portrait of his fiancée, Miss Petra Bain.

'I'm Miss Bain,' Petra said, 'but I'm sure there must be some mistake.'

'No mistake, Miss Bain. Mr. Stoddart was most emphatic. He wanted a painting of you to add to the gallery of family portraits.'

'Oh, dear,' said Petra, 'I'll have to verify this with Mr. Stoddart. You see, he's away from home. No reflection on you, Mr. Reynold, but I must check up that he really meant what he said. May I contact you again?'

Affronted, but trying to hide it, Mr. Reynold agreed to await further instructions.

It was Petra's free day and she wandered round the

house looking for the twins. She found Jay and asked him for Alaric's phone number at his place of work, wherever that was. He had never got round to telling her.

Jay knew and said, 'Don't be surprised if you don't reach him. The man's elusive. He could be anywhere in London. He moves around, he's in demand.'

Petra dialled the number Jay had given her. When she told the telephonist she wished to speak to Mr. Alaric Stoddart, the girl replied at once, as if she were a telephone answering device, 'I'm sorry, he's in conference.'

'But,' Petra protested, 'this is important. Can I get a message to him?'

'Sorry, madam, he's not available.'

'But,' Petra persisted, 'it's essential that I speak to him—'

'Sorry, madam. He won't speak to anyone unless it's an emergency, and then only his immediate family. Or his fiancée. We've had orders.'

In desperation Petra said, 'My name's Petra Bain. I'm his fiancée. Please tell him I want to speak to him.'

'His fiancée, madam? But of course, Miss Bain, if only you'd said . . . I'll put you through at once.'

Someone lifted a receiver, someone said, 'My fiancée? Really?' The voice sounded amused. 'Put her through, will you?' A pause, then 'Petra darling?' The voice was silky smooth.

'Alaric! You know very well I'm not your—'

'But, darling, you've just announced yourself as my fiancée, which proves you are, doesn't it? What does my incomparable fiancée want?'

'She wants you to revoke your order to a Mr. Benedict Reynold to paint her portrait.'

'Ah, now, that's something your husband-to-be absolutely refuses to do. Tradition – Stoddart tradition – demands that I have a portrait painted of my fiancée. You see, my sweet, you now hold a place in Stoddart history. I simply can't let you go unrecorded.'

'But this is ridiculous, Alaric. Not to say a terrible waste of money.'

'It is ridiculous, darling, I grant you that, but it's my

159

money, and I have plenty of it, so if I waste it it's my business. Anyway, some figures in history, and the Stoddarts of the past were no exception, had their mistresses painted in oils and exhibited beside the men they loved! Agreed you aren't my mistress – I've raised you to a higher status than one of those – but convention dictates that Miss Petra Bain must have her portrait painted, which will in due course be hung beside mine in the family picture gallery.'

Petra was appalled and said so.

'Now,' he said tauntingly, 'do you see what you started that day you announced to the local press that you were Alaric Stoddart's wife-to-be?'

She was about to deny it when she realized how useless a denial would be. 'But, Alaric, *please* delay it a little. At least tell the man to wait a bit longer until . . .'

'Until when? If I tell him to wait, you'll be gone. Sorry, Petra, I want that portrait.'

So Petra, with the utmost reluctance, sat for Mr. Benedict Reynold, and the painting was begun. Slowly, startlingly, Petra Bain on canvas came to life. The girl who looked back at her was beautiful, not like the true Petra Bain at all. She was wearing the dress she had worn for the engagement party, the gold draped in glinting folds, her hand resting on the back of a tapestry-covered chair.

Still Alaric stayed away. Petra began to fret. Jay, sensing her disquiet, said they must do something to cheer her up.

'We'll have another party, Jay,' Jenny suggested. 'The four of us, you and Pet, me and Martyn. Where shall it be?' To Petra, 'Didn't Alaric say you could use his apartment?'

'For myself, yes,' Petra answered doubtfully, 'but not for a party.'

'Oh, he'll never know, Pet. If Mrs. Osborn tells him, I'll take the responsibility. If he turns Big Brother, well,' she shrugged, 'that's just too bad.'

But, Petra thought, I'll be the one to take the blame, not you . . .

Jay brought his records, Jenny raided the kitchen for

food under the eyes of a horrified Mrs. Osborn. 'If you make a mess, Miss Jenny,' she said to her and to Petra as they took cups and plates and rolls and cakes, 'in Mr. Stoddart's drawing-room, he'll – he'll skin you alive, you see if he doesn't!'

She spoke as if Jenny were a small girl and Jenny loved it. 'Don't tell Alaric, Mrs. Os,' said Jenny, 'but we're going to dance, too. Pet's fed up, aren't you?' With a knowing smile to the housekeeper, 'She's missing my brother.' Jenny swept out, carrying a tray laden with food and crockery.

In Alaric's sideboard Jay found bottles and Jenny found glasses. Drinks were poured, glasses emptied and refilled. They danced, they ate, they phoned Mrs. Osborn for coffee. Before she could set foot inside the room, Jay took the tray from her, kissed her cheek and pushed her away.

'We'll clear it before we go,' Jenny assured Petra when she grew anxious. 'Come on, Martyn, dance with me.' And willingly Martyn did her bidding. He seemed to have lowered his barriers at last and let Jenny in.

Petra danced with Jay, they turned up the sound until the corridors rang with it. Martyn pulled Jenny on to the couch and kissed her. Petra wondered if he had had too much to drink. Jay was showing signs of over-indulgence, too.

He sat in an armchair and pulled Petra on to his knee. He looked at Jenny and Martyn and said, 'Let's do like-wise, Pet. It's a long time since you've condescended to kiss me – properly. Imagine I'm Alaric and let yourself go.' He pulled her. He abandoned restraint and kissed her with an intensity that made her struggle to get away. He had never kissed her in such a way before.

No one heard the door open, no one knew there was a fifth person in the room until the door slammed shut. The couples broke apart and stared, horrified, into the black anger of the master of Underlings. He looked round, seeing the mess, the empty bottles lying on their sides on the carpet, the half-finished food all over the room. Jenny dived across and switched off the record player.

He said, his voice low with fury, 'Knowing my twin brother and sister, I should have expected something, but never in my life did I expect to find an *orgy* going on in my apartment.' His eyes rested first on Jenny and Martyn, then scathingly on Petra and Jay. 'If you want to continue your debauchery, in the true Stoddart fashion, kindly remove yourselves elsewhere. I suggest the barn, where you can roll in the hay.'

Jenny pulled Martyn out of the room. Jay pushed Petra off his knee, said, 'Sorry, Pet.' To Alaric, 'She's all yours, brother. She never was mine.' He followed the others.

So Petra was left alone to face her fiancée, to take the blame, to clear the mess, to clear herself. She stood, eyes wide with fear, face drained of blood, hands burning and moist, watching him. Stirred to compassion by the shadows round his eyes, the droop of his shoulders, the weary line of his body, she wanted to take him in her arms and comfort him. He was tired, he was tense – and he was white with anger.

This he now turned on Petra. 'And as for *you!*' She flinched under his contempt. 'Why don't you run away like the others? Why don't you follow Jay, my *brave* brother who kisses you, then leaves you like the gentleman he is, to take the brunt of my temper?' His gaze wandered round. 'I gave you permission to use my room, not to *mis*use it. I gave *you* permission to listen to my record player, not to stage a party, nor to indulge in libidinous excesses.'

Once again she couldn't say, 'It wasn't my idea.' She was partly to blame because she hadn't said 'no' to Jenny and Jay. But how could she, in her temporary, false position in the household, tell the brother and sister who really belonged that they had no right to use their brother's apartment, their brother's stereo equipment?

'I've had a long journey. I had trouble with the car. I've had no food or drink for hours. And I come home and find *this*. And you in my brother's arms.' He picked up a half-full bottle, rooted in the sideboard for a clean glass, filled it, threw the contents down his throat and repeated the action with deliberation twice more. The wine, on an empty stomach, was potent.

He went towards her and she backed away. 'I'm sorry, Alaric, I'm really sorry. We didn't expect you home.'

'That was obvious.'

'We were going to clear up the mess. We had no intention of letting you see it like this. We—'

'We, we . . . So you regard yourself as one of the family now, do you? Well, I'll *make* you one of the family.' He caught her wrist and jerked her to him. 'Why should my brother have all your favours and I none? You made yourself my fiancée. I'll make you my—'

He swung her round, pushed her on to the couch and kissed her savagely. His lovemaking was conducted at first with a cold passion, and tears filled her eyes at his heartlessness. Then, when against her will she began to respond, his passion became real and she was torn with anguish. Her love for him was overcoming her resistance, but she knew it was anger, not love for her that was motivating him. If she let him take all that he wanted, she knew she could never hold up her head in front of him – or herself – again.

'Alaric,' she pleaded, 'Alaric, please, *please* stop . . .'

She went slack, unable to resist any more. The circumstances would have to take their course, and if he – a sob escaped her. He raised his head and she was frightened by the look in his eyes. He saw her tears, sat up and put his head in his hands.

'You'd better give me some food.' Her hands were shaking as she picked up a clean plate, collected a couple of rolls and a cake or two and put the plate in front of him. There was some lukewarm coffee in the pot which she poured into a cup. 'You'd better go,' he muttered.

She smoothed her hair, straightened her clothes. 'But Alaric, the mess . . .'

'Mrs. Osborn will clear it.' He raised his head, his eyes infinitely weary. 'For my sake if not your own, will you please *go*!'

'But, Alaric—' If she ran to him now, knelt at his feet, put her arms round him, her head on his lap, what would he do?

She went to the door. She would never know the answer.

Petra heard Alaric come into his room. It was well into the early hours and still she had not slept. She lay there for some time listening to his restless footsteps. There were not the usual sounds of his preparing for bed.

Matters had reached a turning point. Somehow she would have to bring their curious relationship to an end before it was too late. If he ever chose to make love to her again as he had done that evening, and as her fiancé he had every right, she would succumb to his demands, there was no doubt in her mind. Her feeling for him was such that she would want to give in, to give him the pleasure and gratification – however temporary – he sought.

She got out of bed and switched on the light, found her housecoat and stood in front of the communicating door. The key, she noticed, was on her side again. She supposed it was because Yvette had gone and there would be no danger now of the embarrassment of finding them together.

It took a great deal of courage to tap on that door. There was a pause in the unceasing walking up and down, as if Alaric were listening. Petra tapped again and was told to go in.

He was dressed except that his jacket had been removed and his tie loosened. He seemed to have no intention of getting into bed that night.

'What do you want?' His tone was not encouraging.

'To talk to you. I – I can't sleep.'

'I'm sorry if I'm disturbing you.' He spoke coldly.

'It's not that. It's—' She studied the carpet. 'I've decided to look for a job, an acting job.'

'I see.' There was a long pause. 'You wish to be free of me.'

'Yes.' The answer was torn from her.

'When do you want to go? I'll have to arrange for a substitute guide to take your place.'

'Tomorrow – that is, today. As soon as possible.'

'Do you intend to go alone?'

She looked up, surprised. 'Of course. No one else can get a job for me except myself.'

'Where will you stay?'

She shrugged. 'I'll get some digs.'

'You can stay in my suite of rooms. They're in the heart of London.'

'No, thank you. You're under no obligation—'

'But I am. You still wear my ring.' He took a set of keys from his jacket which was thrown across the bed. He gave them to her. She did not dare refuse them. 'There's a resident housekeeper. She'll attend to all your wants.' He stared out into the blackness through his own reflection thrown there by the light behind him. 'Give my address to the theatrical agents you visit. It might help you. Tell them you're going to marry me. I'm well know in many circles, theatrical included. If they're hesitating about whether to offer you a part, your supposed future relationship to me might tip the scales in your favour.'

'It's kind of you, but I'd rather get a job by my own efforts.'

'Even though you've failed in the past?'

'Rest assured,' her voice wavered, but she controlled it, 'I'll do my damnedest to get a part and fulfil your condition for releasing me.'

She returned to bed and slept fitfully until the alarm awoke her. Alaric had breakfasted by the time she went downstairs. She was sorry because she would have liked to have seen him once more. After all, if she was successful in getting a part in a play, she might never see him again. The ring could be returned by post, her belongings packed and sent on to her and that would be the end – the end of an episode, the end of a dream.

Jay bounded into the breakfast room. He kissed her on the cheek. 'Two pieces of news – Jenny's engaged to Martyn!'

Petra's eyes brightened. 'Jay, I'm really glad. How did she manage it?'

'Apparently she put the words into his mouth. You know, a bit like royalty, he didn't like to propose because of her position, so she told him if he ever left Underlings – apparently he's been thinking of it – she'd follow him and find herself an office job near him. He said in that case, if she wasn't going to let him out of her sight, they might as well get married. Would she have him? You can guess the rest!'

'Where is she, Jay? I'd like to congratulate her before I go.'

'You won't find her. She's with Martyn already, planning their "getaway", as she calls it. And here's the other bit of news – you're going to London and I'm going with you. In fact, I'm driving you there in one of Alaric's cars.' He produced a bulging wallet. 'Big Brother's turned benevolent and given me a packet of money. He said look after you and make sure you stay at his flat. Me, too.'

'You're staying there?'

'And going the rounds with you looking for a job myself. Mrs. Os is taking my place as a guide until Alaric can get someone else. She's done it before.' He offered her some toast. 'Pleased to have me with you?'

She had to be honest. 'Delighted,' she said. The prospect of going alone, of trudging from agent to agent, parrying the blows of the shaking heads with no shoulder to weep on, had worried her.

They did not see Alaric before they left. Petra took the disappointment badly. For many miles Jay did the talking. They stopped for lunch and reached London in the late afternoon. Jay knew the way to Alaric's flat, greeted the housekeeper, a slim, smiling, middle-aged woman called Mrs. Rogers, and showed Petra to her bedroom. 'Alaric's,' Jay said. 'His instructions.'

Mrs. Rogers was so pleased to meet Mr. Stoddart's fiancée, she said. She'd heard so much about her from him. He'd told her all about the wonderful party .... 'If there's anything you want, just tell me, Miss Bain.'

Petra and Jay went the round of the theatrical agents. There was no need to walk as they used to, Jay said, or go by bus or Underground. Alaric had given him enough money to hire a taxi just to go next door, if they wanted!

Petra was determined not to use Alaric's name or influence to help her achieve her object, but in the end she tried it, saying she was engaged to him. The only effect it had was to make the agent look at her oddly and say, 'So you're his woman now? I thought he had some fabulous titled model tagging around with him?'

Never again did Petra try to use Alaric's name.

It was pleasant returning to luxury at the end of the day, but after a week Petra had to face facts, she was getting nowhere. The weekend passed slowly. Jay was out, 'making contacts' as he put it. On Monday morning he took Petra to an agent he had been told about by an acquaintance he had made at a party.

'Yes,' said the agent, 'there might be a part for you.' He explained the set-up. 'Come to the audition in the morning, both of you.'

Petra passed the evening alone. She should have been excited, but she was strangely depressed. If she succeeded at last in getting a part, there would be no more Alaric, no more Underlings. When the phone rang, she thought it was Jay. It was Alaric.

He was impersonally interested. 'Getting anywhere?'

'We're making progress. We've both got auditions tomorrow.'

'Congratulations.' The voice was dry.

'I haven't got the part yet.'

'Perhaps not, but if you act as well as you've been acting the part of my wife-to-be, you're in. Where's Jay?'

'Out making contacts.'

'You mean getting drunk.' She didn't answer. 'Which is why I gave him strict instructions to take you around in taxis. I didn't want any more accidents.'

'With your car, I suppose you mean.'

'To hell with my car. It was you I was thinking about.'

'You mean you don't want me to get hurt in case I claim damages against you.'

There was an exasperated pause. 'Obviously London hasn't improved your temper. Are you eating?'

She laughed. 'Reasonably well, thanks to Mrs. Rogers.'

'Good. I gave her strict instructions to supply you with plenty of food.'

'Alaric?' She took a breath. 'If I do get this job, there won't be any need for me to return to Underlings, will there?'

'No.'

'I'll send your ring back by post.'

'Damn the ring!' What was the matter with him? 'I suppose you want me to wish you luck with the audition tomorrow?'

'That's up to you.'

A long pause. 'Well, I won't.'

Another pause. 'Alaric? Goodbye, Alaric.'

The only answer was a click from the other end.

The train drew out of London, moving slowly at first, then speeding on as if glad to shake the dust of the metropolis from its wheels. Petra, sat, head against the side, eyes closed, wondering where her future lay.

The audition had, for her, been a total failure. She had never acted so badly in her life. Afterwards, even Jay asked her what had gone wrong. But her heart hadn't been in it. It had been at Underlings, in the possession of Alaric Stoddart. Perhaps, deep down, Petra reasoned, she hadn't tried very hard because she hadn't wanted the part. To have been given it would have meant being irrevocably parted from the man she loved.

Jay had been luckier. He had been offered the part of understudy to the male lead. He had been overjoyed and had spent the evening and some of the night celebrating. Petra had gone with him, but half-way through the evening, when an attractive redhead had attached herself to Jay, Petra had slipped away and returned to Alaric's flat by taxi. That morning she had packed her case, left a note for Jay who was sleeping off the night's celebrations, thanked Mrs. Rogers for all she had done, and caught the train back to Derbyshire.

When the journey was over and she got out at the

station, she felt she had come home. Instead of taking a hired car, she went on a bus to the village and walked from there.

The early summer evening had a chill about it, but the sky was a clear pale blue. The long, long drive to the house, magnificently sprawling across the green meadows and backed by hill-covered woods, did not tire her feet. Instead, the walk invigorated her. As she approached the great building, it seemed to grow bigger and she felt progressively smaller and insignificant. She compared herself with it like a man standing at the foot of Everest and knew she would never be able to scale the social heights required of the wife of the future owner.

Mrs. Osborn answered the door. She said she was glad to see her back and would she like to wash and join Mr. Stoddart who was dining alone? The housekeeper said would Miss Bain please hurry because the food was getting cold and that would put Mr. Stoddart in a bad mood, which he often was these days . . .

Petra's first instinct was to knock as she stood outside the dining-room door, but she turned the handle and went in. Alaric glanced up, expecting Mrs. Osborn, and saw Petra. He looked for a moment as if he couldn't believe his eyes.

He raised his eyebrows. 'No?' She shook her head. 'Oh. I suppose I should sympathize, say I'm sorry to hear it. Or does that rub salt in the wound?'

She shrugged, unable to speak at the sight of him, fighting an impulse to run over to him and pull his arms about her. He watched her for a moment and patted his shoulder. 'Any good to weep on?'

She smiled tearfully and he pulled out her chair. He asked, 'Where did you lunch?'

'I didn't.'

He seemed quite angry. 'Will you never learn? No wonder you look as though a harsh word would knock you sideways. When is that food coming?'

Mrs. Osborn appeared and apologized for the delay. There was little conversation while they ate, but it was an easy silence. It was as if Alaric was giving her the time to recover from her journey, and perhaps from her disappointment.

Towards the end of the meal, Petra asked, 'Where's Jenny?'

'Gone to stay with Martyn's parents. It's the first time she's met them.'

'I'm so glad they came together at last,' Petra said. 'At least theirs is a happy ending.'

He looked at her curiously from underneath a frown, but merely answered, 'Yes.'

Before they left the dining-room, Alaric directed Petra's attention to the wall over the fireplace. 'An addition to the Stoddart family.'

Petra caught her breath as she saw herself looking back at her, a reflection yet a stranger, placed beside the portrait of Alaric as if she were his equal – and his bride.

'But, Alaric, it's wrong to put me there as if – as if—'

He rested his arm across her shoulders, ignoring her uncertainty. 'The artist did a good job, don't you think?'

'Too good. It makes me beautiful, which I'm not.'

He glanced at her as if to test the sincerity of her words. 'There's a pensiveness about the portrait, a fleeting unhappiness captured almost in spite of itself. Are you unhappy, Petra?'

How could she answer, 'Yes, to my very depths. The artist must be an incredibly perceptive man'? 'Who isn't at times?' she fenced.

He gave a sceptical look. 'Dodging the question?' He led the way into his drawing-room. 'Now, if you were really going to marry me, your portrait would eventually hang beside mine in the State Dining Room.' He poured a drink and gave it to her. 'Any children we might have would in course of time join us.'

She winced as if he had thrust a knife below her ribs. Did he know he was torturing her? He put a record on and as they listened, he sat beside her, except that there was the width of a sprung cushion between them. He closed his eyes and rested his head on the back of the couch. Petra stared pensively into the fire. The music ended, Alaric removed the record.

With his back to her he asked, 'Tell me something, Petra. Why did you come back?'

The question wrecked her composure and started an eruption of doubt. She floundered, 'I – I didn't get a job, did I?'

He threw himself beside her again. 'But I expected you to lie, to tell me you'd got a part whether you had or not, and then return the ring. I have no real claim on you, have I? You're under no obligation to me to remain my fiancée. We signed no contract. It was only a verbal agreement, and people are breaking those every day. So why did you come back?'

Her face burned and she put up her hands to cover it. What was he implying now? That she was after him, wanted his name and status despite all she had said?

Because I love you and couldn't bear to be away from you. The words were in her mind. They would never reach her lips. 'I've – well, I've got a job here, haven't I? You're my employer, you provide me with shelter, food, money . . .'

'I see.' He rose, put a foot on the shining brass fender and stared into the flames. 'Why don't you try the repertory company who run the theatre in the town? I know the management, I support them financially.'

'I'd be wasting my time. Local companies are often tight-knit affairs. Some of them don't seem to welcome newcomers, especially complete unknowns like me.' She laughed without amusement. 'I suppose I could always ask them if they'd employ me to make the tea!'

'When you were in London, did you use my name and give my address?' She murmured 'Yes.'

'And didn't that help?'

'The only remark I got was, "So you're his woman now. What happened to the fabulous titled model he was running around with?" '

Alaric laughed, went across to her and pulled her up, holding her hands. 'Did you mind being called my "woman"?' She lifted her shoulders. 'But you're not, are you?'

'No. And never likely to be.'

He gave a quizzical smile. 'I detect a note of disappointment.' He pulled her close. 'Just say the word, my sweet . . .'

She broke away. 'I'm not good enough for you. I haven't got a title. I'm just plain "Miss". Since the feudal system still applies in this establishment, in the whole Underlings set-up, to you I'm a mere peasant. By your own admission, a Stoddart can dally with a servant-girl, can even give her children, but he must never, ever marry her. Goodnight, Alaric.'

Petra went to bed and cried her heart out. It had been building up all day, and as she lay in the darkness recalling Alaric's question, 'Why did you come back?' the floodgates opened and she sobbed. He was right, she should have returned the ring, anything would have been better than this misery.

It seemed he would be willing to release her now. But, she told herself, be honest, you don't want to be released. From Underlings, perhaps, but not from Alaric Stoddart. He was part of it, of course, and whoever took him would have to take the rest. But it would never be for her to have to make such a momentous decision. Thinking about Alaric as a husband was like someone in a wheelchair gazing longingly at the beckoning summit of a mountain.

A key turned – he must have taken it back while she was away – and the communicating door opened. 'Petra? What's wrong?'

His voice in the darkness was considerate and sympathetic and started the tears again. It would have been better if he'd been brisk and sharp, telling her to pull herself together. She was lying face down and he felt the pillow. It was soaked with her tears. He turned her over, took a handkerchief from his dressing gown and dried her cheeks.

'You must stop. You'll make yourself ill.' He waited while the sobs receded. 'Are you missing Jay?'

'Perhaps.'

'Is it because you didn't find a job?'

If she could put him off the scent by saying yes, then she would say 'Yes'. She mumbled, 'It's no use, I've got to admit I'm a failure. All the time I spent learning to act was wasted. All the money—'

'Your parents' money?'

'No. They had none to spare. I was given a grant by the local authority.' He sat beside her and took her hand. In the darkness he seemed larger than life, so near, yet she couldn't reach out and touch him. If she had taken his hand as he had taken hers, how he would have misinterpreted such an action!

'How long is it since you've had an acting part?'

'Months.'

'But – forgive me if I sound naïve – other girls with relatively little experience manage to get jobs.'

'Of course. Some have ability, real ability – which I haven't. Some have a lot of luck. And others – well, you can surely guess.'

'And you wouldn't sell your soul for a good part in a play?' She wondered if he was laughing at her.

'It wouldn't be my soul I was selling, it would be myself – my self-respect. I have my own standards. I'd have to love someone. Jay often—' She covered her mouth. 'Asked me,' she had nearly said. Which would have been betraying Jay's confidence. When she saw where Alaric's thoughts were leading she almost wished she had.

He stood and thrust his hands into his pockets. 'Well?' His voice had hardened. 'Jay often – what?'

'Forget it.'

'Are you feeling better now?'

'Yes, thank you.' She wished he would go before the tears began again.

'Will you settle down now or would you like me to ring for Mrs. Osborn to bring you some hot milk?'

'No, thank you.' She clenched her fists to hold back the sobs.

He lingered a moment, then returned to his room. Petra, hiding her head under the blankets so as not to disturb him a second time, cried again, with his handkerchief pressed to her cheek. It was still there in the morning when she woke up.

Two days later he told her, 'Good news! I've got you a job.'

Petra put down her knife and fork. She had been dining alone until Alaric came in. She couldn't speak, she couldn't ask 'Where? How?'

He told her. 'You know I've got a financial interest in the local repertory theatre? There's a vacancy for a female lead in the new play they're putting on. I told them all about you, your background, your appearance, your acting ability—'

'Alaric, I can't—'

'Oh, but you can, can't you? Look how excellently you've acted for the past few months. I could hardly fault your performance as my fiancée if I tried. You were so good, there were times when even I believed you might be in love with me.'

'When – when's the audition?'

'No audition. They've taken you on. The play starts its run in a fortnight. Rehearsals begin in two days' time.'

She pushed her plate away. 'But, Alaric, I couldn't—'

'At such short notice? You could. You see, I've even found you a place to live – sharing a flat with one of the women members of the company. You'd take the place of the girl who's left. You'd better start packing in the morning. You've got a lot of clothes to stow away. Take the next two days off, with pay.' He smiled. 'Consider yourself fired from then on, Miss Bain. Your services to Underlings – and to me – will no longer be required. The condition I imposed has been complied with.' He pushed her plate in front of her. 'Eat, girl, with a clear conscience. You're free of me at last.'

Petra picked up her knife and fork. She had to force herself to eat, otherwise her misery would show. She forced a smile, too, as well as an appetite. Her eyes lit up like a stage at the start of a performance. She said she was overjoyed. By heaven, she congratulated herself, if I've never acted before, I'm acting now.

The internal phone rang. Alaric answered. 'Put him

through to my office, Mrs. Osborn, will you?' To Petra, 'Jay. You'd better come with me. You'll want to tell him the news yourself.'

In the office he picked up the phone. 'Alaric here.' He listened. 'You have? Where? Good idea. Yvette? What about her?' Petra picked up a pencil, twisted it round and round. 'Has she now?' Alaric's tone was cynical. 'Leave the keys with Mrs. Rogers. Keep the car for the moment. But keep it intact. Stay sober while you're driving it. Pet?' He turned. 'Yes, she's here.' He took the pencil from her fingers. 'Getting very agitated. She's got some news to tell you.'

'Jay? Alaric's got me a job. Local rep. They want me to play the female lead.'

'Pet! Aren't you excited?'

She forced enthusiasm into her reply. I'm delighted, Jay. Can't believe it. Come and see me there?'

'Try and stop me! Been telling Alaric I've found myself a couple of rooms. Got fed up with Yvette phoning to ask why Alaric wasn't in town.'

So Yvette was on Alaric's trail again. But had she ever lost his scent, even through the whole period of the mock engagement?

'How did you make out with that redhead the other evening, Jay?'

'Made great strides, Pet! What happened to you?'

'I felt superfluous. I didn't want to get in your way.' A pause. 'I'd never stand in the way of any man who wanted another woman.' Involuntarily she looked up and saw Alaric's raised eyebrows.

'Darling,' the voice came over loud and clear, 'what man could ever want another woman when you're around? Why did you walk out of my life without so much as a farewell kiss?'

'I decided to leave you to sleep it off.' What would Alaric make of that statement? 'I had a living to earn, remember? Underlings called.'

'Only Underlings, Pet?' She pressed her lips tightly together. He must have guessed what her reaction would be because he laughed. 'Well, you can turn your back on the place and its heir now you're top of the bill. 'Bye, love. See you on stage.'

'Come back to my apartment, Petra,' said Alaric.

Remembering the part she had to play in front of her host, she drew back her shoulders, threw off her depression and followed him, exuberant, into the drawing-room.

He turned towards her. 'A noticeable omission. You haven't thanked me yet.'

Her eyes shone, she scintillated, vying in brilliance with the chandeliers overhead. 'I do thank you, Alaric. What a wonderful break!'

He looked at her reflectively, narrowly, and she wondered if she were overdoing it. But it was vital, she told herself, to convince him of her pleasure, her unbounded delight at getting a part at last – and breaking free of him. 'I'll try not to let you down, Alaric,' she rushed on. 'The female lead! It's like a dream! Will you come and see me when the show opens?'

'I wouldn't miss the performance for the world,' he said dryly.

He put on some music – a violin concerto, by Max Bruch, she guessed – and as she listened to the poignant, infinitely stirring harmonies, her head dropped back and her eyes closed. She thought of her parents. She longed for the sight of them of their cottage, her small room under the sloping roof with a tiny casement window you could lean against and look towards the northern hills and imagine yourself wandering in their stillness and solitude.

If she were there she might lose for a time the unhappiness that clung to her, close as her own shadow, never letting go . . .

Petra did not realize the music had ended until Alaric spoke. 'Where were you?'

Her face leapt from repose to exhilaration. 'Can't you guess? I was onstage, seeing myself as the leading lady.' She clasped her hands. 'You probably won't believe it's something I've dreamed about ever since I started learning to act.'

He turned sideways in his seat to watch her. 'You

have? So it's a lifetime's ambition I've helped you achieve?'

She put her hand over his. 'I honestly don't know how to thank you, Alaric.'

He slid his hand from her grasp and clasped her fingers instead. 'There's a way,' he said with a touch of sarcasm, 'but you couldn't do it, not without losing your self-respect.'

She laughed gaily, throwing her head back against the cushions. I must remember, she thought, when I'm back in my own room, to pat myself on the back. I give myself full marks for this piece of acting. It's a one-night performance, never to be repeated.

He went across to the sideboard, poured two drinks and put one in her hand. 'Let us drink to your future.' He lifted his glass and touched hers. 'To Petra Bain, star of the show, and to her exceptional acting ability. May she long continue to charm her audiences and show them exactly what she's made of.'

'And to you, Alaric, for getting me this wonderful job.'

As she drank, she felt his eyes on her, but she would not look at him. He took her glass. 'Now, Miss Bain, we must say goodbye.'

For a petrifying second her mask slipped. Her hand went to her hair in an effort to cover her face. As she pretended to tidy straying strands, she recovered her poise. She summoned a smile. 'You're going away?'

'Yes. Tomorrow, to London.' Of course, Petra thought, Yvette ... When his lady-friend called, Alaric went. What was there to stop him? No imitation wife-to-be hanging round his neck. 'I shall leave early, before breakfast. I won't see you again, except as a member of your audience. If I can fight my way through throngs of admirers, I might even visit you backstage. In your star dressing-room.' He put out his hand and she put hers into it.

'Thank you, Alaric, for – for everything.' Was this the end? No more than a handshake? I must smile, she told herself, whatever I do in the privacy of my bedroom, I *must* smile now.

She went to the door. 'Goodbye, Alaric.' She opened the door.

'Petra? Haven't you forgotten something?'

She frowned. 'Have I?'

'The ring?'

The ring, still on her engagement finger!

'History repeating itself?' he asked mockingly. 'Remember the first time we became "engaged"? The morning in the hotel? You forgot to "disengage" yourself from me then.'

She coloured deeply. 'I'm so sorry.' She pulled off the ring which was traditionally worn by the brides-to-be of the Stoddart heirs. Would it now pass to Lady Yvette?

'Think nothing of it,' he commented dryly.

She placed the ring in his open palm. For a second their eyes met, then she left him.

CHAPTER TEN

PETRA got up late, having slept heavily after a restless night. She breakfasted alone, then she told Mrs. Osborn not to bother to provide lunch. She would be packed and left before then. Yes, she was going for good. She'd got a job, an acting job in the town. Didn't Mrs. Osborn know?

Mrs. Osborn said, turning pale, 'But Mr. Stoddart? What about him? He'll miss you so, Miss Bain.' She looked at Petra's empty hand.

Petra coloured. 'It – it didn't work, Mrs. Osborn. We're not engaged any more. I thought Mr. Stoddart would have told you.'

'My dear, I'm so sorry. And after that wonderful party, too. Are you *sure* it's over? Isn't there any chance—?'

'None at all, Mrs. Osborn. You've been so kind to me.' Spontaneously she hugged the woman, who patted Petra's shoulder and left her, tears in her eyes.

Petra thought, I mustn't look back. I must do what I'm going to do without questioning the sense of it, whether it's right or wrong. She took a hired car to the town, having refused the chauffeur's offer to take her there. Her baggage was light because she was taking no more than she had arrived with. The beautiful clothes Alaric had paid for were left hanging in the wardrobe.

She went into a public phone box, found the number of the theatre and rang it. The message she gave was, 'Miss Bain was sorry but she had unavoidably been called away. She wouldn't be joining the cast, she was leaving the district.'

Half an hour later, she was in the train speeding north. She was going home. She would forget about acting and find a secretarial job. She would forget – in time – Underlings and all that Alaric had stood for. Would she ever forget him? Never, she thought, although she would slip out of his mind like a handful of water falling back into the sea. Today he had Yvette. Perhaps tomorrow, some other woman might take Yvette's place, the day after, yet another. An ocean of woman . . .

She arrived on her parents' doorstep almost ill with misery and fatigue. Her mother was there, her arms raised invitingly and a haven, grey-haired, amply built, her apron telling of things like washing and cooking and clearing. Petra realized how much she had missed the everyday simplicities of life.

'What's the matter, Petra? Tell me, dear.' She lifted Petra's hand. 'No ring? No engagement? Didn't it work out?'

Petra could only shake her head. 'Don't ask me about it now, Mum. I'll tell you soon. Not now, not now . . .'

'I'll get you a cup of tea, dear. Sit down, take off your coat.'

In the small, simply furnished living-room, Petra sank on to a chair and let the peace and serenity of home flow over her like a warm bath, easing the pain from her mind. Here Underlings seemed unreal, remote and utterly artificial, a place to look round, admire from a distance, perhaps even, momentarily, to covet a little as she had done once, long ago, as she had wandered round the grounds with Alaric by her side.

It was in the darkness of the night that Underlings became real again. The face of Alaric Stoddart stood out, like the sweeping beam of a lighthouse, in the blackness of her mind. She had told her parents the truth, that it had never been a real engagement, that Alaric had never loved her, that circumstances had forced her into posing as his fiancée until sufficient time had elapsed for the engagement to be considered broken. Her parents had taken it sadly, but well. They had wanted the best for their daughter, her father, a quiet, understanding man, had said. They had wanted her to marry well and not have to skimp and scrape as they had done.

Petra found herself a job in an insurance office. The work was not inspiring, but it was well paid. She spent her spare time walking on the moors, taking her tea and trudging miles until she was exhausted, trying all the time to purge herself of her longing for Alaric Stoddart.

It was harder than she had thought. Now and then she would feel for his ring and an involuntary shudder of fear would shake her each time she discovered her finger was bare. Then she would remember, it wasn't meant to be there, she hadn't lost it after all. She had only lost the man who had given it to her.

It was summer now and the evenings were long, twilight coming late. Petra wore slacks and open-necked blouse; her rucksack hung from her shoulder and she felt at peace. The moors were a medicine, they were working their magic. Lying back on the slopes, staring into the sky, listening to the curlews call, she could bear to think of the future, a future without the man she loved.

Six weeks had passed since they had said goodbye, six weeks on the calendar, six years measured in her mind's time. She walked down the hill towards the village, still with a Sunday evening quiet. Tomorrow, Monday, work again. And so it would go on into the future, working and walking, stuffy office alternating with the sweeping, endless moors . . .

A figure climbed the hill. It was distant and small and as it came nearer it grew larger and turned into a man. A man was climbing with firmness and determination, a stranger to the area, yet not a stranger to her sight.

Her heart stopped, throbbed and raced and her mind said, 'It's an illusion. It's my eyes fooling me, turning every man in Alaric Stoddart . . . But it *was* Alaric Stoddart. Wasn't it? No other man had that physique, that proud way of holding his head, that thick straying hair, those dark, keen eyes.

He stood in front of her, barring her way. 'Petra?' He was dressed as he had been the first time she had met him, roll-necked shirt, fawn cord jacket and trousers. With all her being she wanted to cry, 'Go away!' You mustn't be allowed to re-open old wounds. They've just started to heal a little.

'You were passing through the area, you're going to say. Thought you'd call and see me, say "*Hallo*" and pass on your way.' Then it struck her that he hadn't known her address, must in fact have gone to some lengths to find it.

He gave a strained, tired smile. 'Have you forgotten me? Already?'

'*Forgotten* you?' She cursed the emphasis on the vital word, giving away, in a subtle, spontaneous way, without even saying the words, 'How could I *ever* forget Alaric Stoddart?'

She took refuge in the commonplace. 'How did you know where to find me?'

'I called on your parents.' He told her what she already knew. 'You can see this hill from your cottage. They pointed you out as you walked down towards the village. Every Sunday, they said, and most evenings you walk miles across the moors. Alone.'

The last word was almost a challenge. 'I love the moors,' she said defensively, 'as much as you love Underlings.' She looked at him. 'This is my true environment, Alaric.'

He gazed around as if trying to feel what she felt, see with her eyes, the grandeur, so different from the grandeur of Underlings, the beauty, so different from the contrived beauties of his home. 'And nothing would take its place? Nothing could ever take you away?'

'Why should it? It's where I was brought up, where I'll live, probably where I'll die.' If, she added to herself, I haven't died already.

He smiled a little. 'So melancholy? You sound depressed. Why?'

She turned away and sat on the ground, hoping the action would divert his thoughts. But he said again, as he took his place beside her, 'Why, Petra?' She was silent. 'Why did you run away?'

She tried again to sidetrack. 'Who told you where I lived?'

'Jay remembered the name of the village but not the address. I found the place on the map, drove up here, booked in at the village pub. They knew your parents. Petra, why did you run away?'

'Why have you come?' she cried with passion, unable any longer to keep her emotions under control. 'To delve, to ask questions I refuse to answer?'

He was silent for a long time. Then, 'Would it help,' he asked the hills above the village, 'if I told you I loved you? That I want you to marry me? Would it help if I told you I've passed an unbearable six weeks away from you, that you haven't been out of my mind for a single moment since we parted? That I didn't know you'd gone because for six weeks I made myself stay away from you, before returning to Underlings and phoning you at the theatre, only to be told you'd turned down the offer, saying you'd been "called away"?' His voice softened. 'Would it help if I told you I fell in love with you the moment I saw your pale, tired face in Jay's car, looking up at me with a mute appeal, a sort of hunger – and something very like fear?'

He leaned over her. 'Are you afraid of me, Petra?' He turned her face towards him, pushing back her hair. 'Open your eyes, my darling. Look at me again, let me read your answer in your face.'

She looked at him and he saw all he needed to see. His arms lifted her, crushing her to him. His lips covered hers, drawing her love into him as if he needed it to enable him to go on living. There were tears in her eyes, of relief and happiness and he kissed those away.

'The night I met you,' he murmured against her lips, 'the night we spent in the car, with you in my arms, I discovered heaven on earth. I also discovered that it couldn't be bought, that for the first time in my life a woman wasn't mine for the asking. The woman I desired for love and not merely for passing pleasure.'

'I remember you said heaven "couldn't be bought",' she whispered. 'I wondered what you meant.'

'The way you turned down every offer of money I made, every inducement I waved in front of you like a carrot. My darling, if you had given me what I tried to get out of you that morning at the hotel I would have taken it, but I think I might have hated you as well as loved you for it.' He kissed her passionately. 'Heaven,' he went on, 'was the day I discovered you had become "engaged" to me and,' he covered her mouth with his hand as she began to speak, 'I knew it was Jay and not you who told the press. But I wanted you to think I didn't believe him when he told me because I would have had to let you go. And I never wanted to let you go. So I imposed the condition.'

'Thinking I was such a bad actress,' she said indignantly, 'that I'd never manage to get myself a job?'

He laughed. 'On the contrary, I thought you'd given such a good performance as my fiancée, I was afraid you *would* get one – until the evening I told you I'd got you that part in the play. Then, my sweet, I really saw you act and then I began to wonder. And hope.'

She smoothed his hair. 'What did you hope?'

'That you'd turn the job down and say you'd rather stay on at Underlings with me. But you didn't, so I went away.'

'To Yvette.'

'No. I sent Yvette away. Since I met you, she's played no part in my life at all – except, I must admit, to help make you jealous! Satisfied?' She nodded contentedly. 'I could, of course, act the jealous lover myself and ask "What about my brother?"'

She laughed. 'Don't you remember Jay once said, "She's yours, brother. She never has been mine"? He was right.'

She pressed closer to him and his arms tightened. 'You realise, Pet, what you're taking on? I warned you once that I'd be a demanding husband. Will you mind?'

Her answer was to reach out to him and revel in his delighted response to her action.

He murmured against her hair, 'The ancestor who built the Temple of Achilles was right. We Stoddarts all have our vulnerable spot and, beloved, the moment we met you found mine.'

A long time later he said, 'After we're married we'll come and stay with your parents.'

'You don't mind,' she asked shyly, 'that we live in such a modest house? After Underlings, the cottage is so small you can hardly turn round in it!'

'Why should I mind, my darling? I've seen your bedroom,' he said against her ear. 'It's small, yes, but I love it. And why? Because when we come to stay and we share it, you'll have to get all the closer to me!'

She kissed him for that.

He became serious and said, 'You know Underlings belongs to my father? Which means I can't hand it to the National Trust, it isn't mine to give. One day it will be, then I'll do whatever you wish. But even if we – we, my love – were to give it to the Trust, you know they would allow us to continue living there? That they prefer the original owners and their families to go on occupying these great houses because it makes them into living things and prevents them from becoming mere museums? Will you mind that too much, Petra?'

'No, Alaric,' she whispered. 'It's your home and if you love it as much as I love mine, I'd never dream of taking you away from it. And Alaric,' she hid her face against him, 'I'll do my best to grow into the sort of woman you want me to be.'

'Then stay as you are, my sweet, that's all I ask.'

He took the engagement ring from his pocket. 'You see, I had the foresight to bring it with me.' He slipped it on to her finger. 'This time our engagement is real. By the way,' he added casually but smiling, 'your parents are delighted. I got their consent before I came to meet you.'

She laughed at his arrogance. 'Were you so sure of me?'

'No, just hopeful. You remember you told me soon after we met that if you loved a man and thought he didn't love you, you'd never tell him? Instead, you would run as far away from him as you could? It was that thought, my sweet, that spurred me on as I drove up here today. You ran away from me, a long, long way. Did it, I wondered, mean you loved me? Which is why I was so hopeful. Incidentally, before we leave here the day after tomorrow you're going to marry me.'

She sat up. 'I am?'

He patted his pocket. 'The special licence. You'll have to marry me because I'm taking you back to Underlings and since I've booked a room for two at a luxury hotel half-way home, you'll either have to come as my wife or my "woman", as someone called you.'

She lay down and murmured as his lips sought hers again, 'The two can't be separated, so make it both. Your woman and your wife.' She sighed, relaxing into his arms. 'I'm so glad I can stop acting. It was terrible having to pretend I loved you when all the time I really did love you.'

He laughed and told her to stop talking nonsense and let him give her a practical demonstration of the warmth and the passion the Stoddarts, both past and present, were capable of showing to the woman they loved.

Which he proceeded to do to her complete and lasting satisfaction.

THE OMNIBUS
Has Arrived!

A GREAT NEW IDEA
From HARLEQUIN

OMNIBUS — The **3** in **1** HARLEQUIN
only $1.50 per volume

Here is a great new exciting idea from Harlequin.
THREE GREAT ROMANCES — complete and
unabridged — BY THE SAME AUTHOR — in one
deluxe paperback volume — for the unbelievably
low price of only $1.50 per volume.

We have chosen some of the finest works of four
world-famous authors . . .

> VIOLET WINSPEAR
> ISOBEL CHACE
> JOYCE DINGWELL
> SUSAN BARRIE

. . . and reprinted them in the 3 in 1 Omnibus.
Almost 600 pages of pure entertainment for just
$1.50 each. A TRULY "JUMBO" READ!

These four Harlequin Omnibus volumes are now
available. The following pages list the exciting
novels by each author.

Climb aboard the Harlequin Omnibus now! The
coupon below is provided for your convenience in
ordering.

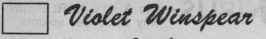

Violet Winspear
Omnibus

"To be able to reproduce the warmly exciting world of romance . . . a colourful means of escape", this was the ambition of the young VIOLET WINSPEAR, now a world famous author. Here, we offer three moving stories in which she has well and truly achieved this.

. . . . CONTAINING

PALACE OF THE PEACOCKS . . . where we join young Temple Lane, in the ridiculous predicament of masquerading as a youth on an old tub of a steamer, somewhere in the Java Seas. She had saved for five years to join her fiancee in this exotic world of blue skies and peacock waters — and now . . . she must escape him . . . (#1318).

BELOVED TYRANT . . . takes us to Monterey, where high mountainous country is alive with scents and bird-song above the dark blue surge of the Pacific Ocean. Here, we meet Lyn Gilmore, Governess at the Hacienda Rosa, where she falls victim to the tyranny of the ruthless, savagely handsome, Rick Corderas . . . (#1032).

COURT OF THE VEILS . . . is set in a lush plantation on the edge of the Sahara Desert, where Roslyn Brant faces great emotional conflict, for not only has she lost all recollection of her fiancee and her past, but the ruthless Duane Hunter refuses to believe that she ever was engaged to marry his handsome cousin . . . (#1267).

$1.50 per volume

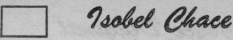

Isobel Chace
Omnibus

A writer of romance is a weaver of dreams. This is true of ISOBEL CHACE, and her many thousands of ardent readers can attest to this. All of her eagerly anticipated works are so carefully spun, blending the mystery and the beauty of love.

. . . . CONTAINING

A HANDFUL OF SILVER . . . set in the exciting city of Rio de Janeiro, with its endless beaches and tall skyscraper hotels, and where a battle of wits is being waged between Madeleine Delahaye, Pilar Fernandez the lovely but jealous fiancee of her childhood friend, and her handsome, treacherous cousin — the strange Luis da Maestro . . . (#1306).

THE SAFFRON SKY . . . takes us to a tiny village skirting the exotic Bangkok, Siam, bathed constantly in glorious sunshine, where at night the sky changes to an enchanting saffron colour. The small nervous Myfanwy Jones realizes her most cherished dream, adventure and romance in a far off land. In Siam, two handsome men are determined to marry her — but, they both have the same mysterious reason . . . (#1250).

THE DAMASK ROSE . . . in Damascus, the original Garden of Eden, we are drenched in the heady atmosphere of exotic perfumes, when Vickie Tremaine flies from London to work for Perfumes of Damascus and meets Adam Templeton, fiancee of the young rebellious Miriam, and alas as the weeks pass, Vickie only becomes more attracted to this your Englishman with the steel-like personality . . . (#1334).

$1.50 per volume

Joyce Dingwell

Omnibus

JOYCE DINGWELL'S lighthearted style of writing and her delightful characters are well loved by a great many readers all over the world. An author with the unusual combination of compassion and vitality which she generously shares with the reader, in all of her books.

. . . . CONTAINING

THE FEEL OF SILK . . . Faith Blake, a young Australian nurse becomes stranded in the Orient and is very kindly offered the position of nursing the young niece of the Marques Jacinto de Velira. But, as Faith and a young doctor become closer together, the Marques begins to take an unusual interest in Faith's private life . . . (#1342).

A TASTE FOR LOVE . . . here we join Gina Lake, at Bancroft Bequest, a remote children's home at Orange Hills, Australia, just as she is nearing the end of what has been a very long "engagement" to Tony Mallory, who seems in no hurry to marry. The new superintendent, Miles Fairland however, feels quite differently as Gina is about to discover . . . (#1229).

WILL YOU SURRENDER . . . at Galdang Academy for boys, "The College By The Sea", perched on the cliff edge of an Australian headland, young Gerry Prosset faces grave disappointment when her father is passed over and young Damien Manning becomes the new Headmaster. Here we learn of her bitter resentment toward this young man — and moreso, the woman who comes to visit him . . . (#1179).

$1.50 per volume

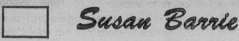

Susan Barrie
Omnibus

The charming, unmistakable works of SUSAN BARRIE, one of the top romance authors, have won her a reward of endless readers who take the greatest of pleasure from her inspiring stories, always told with the most enchanting locations.

. . . . CONTAINING

MARRY A STRANGER . . . Doctor Martin Guelder sought only a housekeeper and hostess for his home, Fountains Court, in the village of Herfordshire in the beautiful English countryside. Young Stacey Brent accepts his proposal, but soon finds herself falling deeply in love with him — and she cannot let him know . . . (#1043).

THE MARRIAGE WHEEL . . . at Farthing Hall, a delightful old home nestled in the quiet countryside of Gloucestershire, we meet Frederica Wells, chauffeur to Lady Allerdale. In need of more financial security, Frederica takes a second post, to work for Mr. Humphrey Lestrode, an exacting and shrewd businessman. Almost immediately — she regrets it . . . (#1311).

ROSE IN THE BUD . . . Venice, city of romantic palaces, glimmering lanterns and a thousand waterways. In the midst of all this beauty, Catherine Brown is in search of the truth about the mysterious disappearance of her step-sister. Her only clue is a portrait of the girl, which she finds in the studio of the irresistably attractive Edouard Moroc — could it be that he knows of her whereabouts? . . . (#1168).

$1.50 per volume